with **JUHI CHAWLA**

EPIC Television Channel is the flagship factual entertainment offering from IN10 Media—a network with diverse interests in the media and entertainment sector. It is an India-centric, content-driven destination that has redefined the genre by being the only native Hindi-language infotainment channel. With a reputation for excellence in showcasing premium factual content that celebrates, explores, discovers and inspires India through untold stories, facts and possibilities, over the years, EPIC Television Channel has been bestowed with several accolades, including the prestigious PromaxBDA Award across various categories, the Indian Television Academy Award for the show *Stories by Rabindranath Tagore* and the Asian Rainbow Television Award for the show *Umeed India.*

Sharanam

with **JUHI CHAWLA**

A Journey in Faith

Published by
Rupa Publications India Pvt. Ltd 2019
7/16, Ansari Road, Daryaganj
New Delhi 110002

Sales centres:
Allahabad Bengaluru Chennai
Hyderabad Jaipur Kathmandu
Kolkata Mumbai

ISBN: 978-93-5333-616-5

First impression 2019

10 9 8 7 6 5 4 3 2 1

Transcribed and translated by Malobika Chatterjee

CONTENTS

1

KAMAKHYA TEMPLE

Perched on top of Nilachal Hills in Guwahati lies a temple that is one of the most revered shrines of Ma Kali in India—the Kamakhya Devi Temple. Steeped in mythical history, this temple is one of the oldest and most revered Shakti peeths and, according to one legend, named after the God of Love, Kamadeva. The Kamakhya Devi Temple is a unique temple that celebrates the power and divinity of womanhood. In this chapter, we take you on a journey to experience the divine energy that pulls the faithful into its holy embrace. Witness the power and faith that evokes the most basic as well as the most profound prayer in the heart of the devout.

Juhi Chawla: When there was nothing, He was omnipresent. When there will be utter emptiness, He will still be there. For aeons, people have an ingrained belief that there is a mystical power that has tied together so many millions of people. Sometimes with hands raised in faith and sometimes with hands folded in obeisance; sometimes carrying thalis of holy offerings, and at others, bearing the holy books in

faith—through these, all of us are engaged in a continual search for Him.

I, Juhi Chawla, will take you on such a sojourn, which is a unification of all such feelings, which traverses thousands of miles and draws people to the places where we may find Him. The experience of that faith, this journey, is of the conviction that we will.

Strength or power is a form of creation. This is the supreme consciousness, supreme knowledge. This is the fundamental energy. She is the Goddess, She is the Mother. And devotees throng here and express themselves in various ways:

Devotee 1: Ever since my childhood, I have been hearing tales about this place from my mother.

Devotee 2: Received very powerful, energetic vibrations from this place.

Devotee 3: This is a very pious place.

Devotee 4: I have regained life here.

Devotee 5: Whatever is asked from the deity here is obtained, without a shred of doubt.

Devotee 6: One feels like coming here time and time again.

Devotee 7: All devotees from across the world offer prayers here.

Devotee 8: There is no peace...one has to find peace within oneself.

Devotee 9: I am from Nepal.

Devotee 10: I am from Jorigram, Dehradun, Uttarakhand.

Devotee 11: We are from Bengaluru.

Devotee 12: I have been coming here for forty to forty-two years.

Devotee 13: I have been coming for about seven years.

Devotee 14: Discharge all your negative energies and go in peace from here.

Juhi Chawla: To the northeast of India, on the southern coast of the Brahmaputra, lies Guwahati, in the state of Assam. Guwahati is surrounded by mountains on all sides. But to the west lie the Nilachal Hills, which have a special eminence attached to it. On this mountain is situated an ancient and extremely powerful temple—the Kamakhya Temple. The one that fulfils all desire is Kamakhya, the one who grants you wishes.

Since the Nilachal Hills are associated with the gemstone neelam (blue sapphire), naturally Shani, or Saturn, is strongly prevalent there. If Saturn is prevalent, then quite naturally, tantra is also practised there. Positive energy is absorbed and negativity diminishes, resulting in an illuminated life. It is widely believed that no matter what religion a person follows, anyone can approach the Mother. She is the Mother of the entire universe and every human here is Her child.

Devotee 15: If someone is able to receive Her blessings, then he is saved. Whenever there's any trouble or danger, some solution or the other will come to the fore. The danger will pass.

Devotee 16: My son was pursuing engineering, and when the campus job fair was about to take place, I went to the Divine Mother. I prayed to Her to let him be selected. He was selected.

Devotee 17: I could not walk and I would have to climb the stairs every day. I had a lot of faith in Her and kept praying—please allow me to come to You, please allow me to come to You.

Devotee 18: If there is pain, it does not matter, I will go.

Juhi Chawla: This is a belief. When one reaches the mountains in the intoxication of this belief, he/she will not return empty-handed from the Mother's shrine. Devotees believe that the place is not so much a place of 'darshan' as it is a place of feeling recharged.

In the Hindu religious Kaalika Purana text, it is clearly stated that Ma Kamakhya is none other than Ma Kali Herself. She destroys all sin and drives away all problems besetting life. We are all Her children, part of Her.

Devotee 19: Come here any day and circle around the shrine of Mother Kamakhya. Make an offering of flowers to Her and then just observe what blessings are bestowed on you.

Devotee 20: People come here and empty out all emotional turmoil in them. When devotees step inside the temple, they are infused with inner strength.

Devotee 21: Walking around the Kamakhya mountains is believed to enhance the holy nature of the place. Above the Kamakhya mountains is the centre of the universe, its navel. Thus the importance of this place.

Juhi Chawla: Here a mystical love story is also prevalent—the love story of Ma Sati and Lord Shiva, which is the pride and foundation of this pious land.

When Sati's father, Daksharaja, had arranged a yajna, he had invited all the gods and goddesses but not Lord Shiva. Sati wanted to attend this, but Shiva refused to permit it. This greatly upset Sati, so much so that Shiva agreed to allow Her to go. When at the yajna, Sati asked Her father the reason for not inviting Shiva, he spoke about Shiva in a very insulting manner. Sati was greatly shamed and self-immolated in the yajna fire. Lord Shiva, being omniscient, got to know what had happened. He opened his eyes wide and plucked out just a strand of hair from His head and cast it on the ground. A demon named Veerbhadra was created, who destroyed everything. Then Shiva appeared and, with the dead body of Sati, began dancing in a frenzy of rage. All the gods then prayed to Lord Vishnu to do something to stop the chaos. Lord Vishnu used His chakra to dismember the body of Sati. As Shiva continued His dance of rage, Sati's body parts began to fall in various parts of the Earth. Wherever each part fell became known as a scared place. Of all the parts that were dismembered, Sati's yoni (a woman's most private part) fell here, in Kamakhya.

Sati's shame at Her husband being insulted by Her father, and Shiva's rage and frenetic dance of rage at His wife's death, are reflected in the images carved on the walls of the temple— they depict the love story of Shiva and Sati.

It is from the point that Sati's yoni fell that the holy water flows. That is why it is considered to be divine nectar.

Devotee 22: I pay my respects in all temples, but the greatness of Kamakhya is not just gazing at the Goddess but touching and feeling Her presence.

Devotee 23: If you drink the divine nectar, there will be no rebirth for you—that is to say you will attain moksha. When I partake of this, it seems to me that I have been blessed by the Mother.

Devotee 24: I have drunk the divine nectar and have unwavering faith that I will attain moksha.

Juhi Chawla: Ma is the fundamental or Adi Shakti. She is the Ultimate Power, the Greatest Power. If the protective umbrella of Her kindness is above us, life's sorrows, problems and worries can never get close. Whatever the situation we are in, good or bad, our devotion should always be for Her.

Devotee 25: There must be devotion to God. There is no end to the might of the Divine. The name does not matter, it can be anything—Kali, Tara, Bagala, Kamala or Bhairavi. Then there is Dhumavati, Bhuvaneswari, Matangi and Chinnmasta.

Juhi Chawla: Thousands of pilgrims come here every day to bow their heads in obeisance. There is hope that the Mother, who is the symbol of knowledge, power, cheer and prosperity, will fill their lives with joy. But why did Kamakhya come to be so named? There is an epic story related to this. After the death of Sati, Shiva sat immersed in deep meditation. Seeing this, the gods sent Kamdev to disrupt Shiva's meditation. Just as his arrow of flowers touched Shiva, His meditation broke. This angered Him so much that with one mere glance, He turned Kamdev to ashes. This took place at a distance of about 35 km from the Kamakhya Temple, at Madan Kamdev Temple, where the remnants of a temple can still be seen today.

When Shiva had destroyed Kamdev, his wife had begged for his life. Then Shiva had asked her to build a temple at the Shakti Peeth there. It was on her request that Vishwakarma built the Kamakhya temple, which means the renowned goddess of desire. That is why this is called Kamakhya.

Kamakhya has always been a vital pilgrimage centre for Hindus, particularly for those practising tantra.

Kamakhya Devi is a place of power, or Shaktisthan. Here, it is mainly tantra that is followed and tantra worship that is carried out. Just as there is the Vedic type of worship, there is tantra worship. Kamakhya is a muktasthan (a place where you attain freedom).

An ambiance of eclipse prevails here throughout, during which period any devotional prayer through tantra, mantra or any other form bears fruit and positive results.

Devotee 26: Initially, there were a lot of misconceptions about Kamakhya. People were scared to come here because they believed that through occult practices people would be turned into sheep, cows or goats. There is nothing like that.

Devotee 27: Tantric worship is carried out here, sometimes for ten days—I am not very clear about that. But practising tantra is fruitful for worshippers.

Devotee 28: It is a very ancient temple. Even my grandfather said that it is a very powerful temple and that everybody goes to pray there.

Devotee 29: The Kamakhya Temple is a major pilgrimage

centre of Goddess Parvati. Anybody who comes here has their prayers fulfilled, if done genuinely from the heart.

Juhi Chawla: The Kamakhya Temple was destroyed a number of times due to outside attacks. But one thing that has been found to remain the same from the beginning is the half-finished, dilapidated flight of stairs. There is also a tale in connection with the origin of these stairs in the Nilachal Hills. It is the story of the demon Narakasur and his love for the Mother.

There was a demon by the name of Narakasur. He was a very volatile and dangerous demon. Kamakhya Devi was so beautiful that Narakasur was determined to marry her. But Bhagwati put some conditions before him. The Goddess asked him to construct a staircase from the terrain. No sooner had he begun and completed the first stair, than the Goddess realized that at this rate, Narakasur would complete constructing the staircase before sunset. So she took the form of a cock and crowed before it was sunrise. Bhagwati used her powers to thwart Narakasur's efforts. And taking the opportunity, Bhagwati killed him.

Devotee 30: Ma Kamakhya, who is also known as Mahamaya, is the prime source of energy or power! She is also the paramount inspiration in the process of creation of the universe. That is why She can also be worshipped in the form of a pre-puberty girl.

Devotee 31: It is the norm here that if you come here, a young girl will have to be worshipped. The worship of the girl child done out of respect for Ma Kamakhya is a pious and potent form of worship, performed according to Vedic norms. Because one never knows when and in the form of which girl Ma will make an appearance. Girls from the age of two to nine are regarded as a form of Shakti, or strength. Devotees who come here need not go for a very elaborate worship, but worshipping a girl child is a must. They can obtain the blessings of the Mother in this manner.

Devotee 32: The greatness of the Mother and the fame of the temple people have come to understand very well. They return here time and again, and some devotees even stay back year after year.

Devotee 33: I have a friend who comes here every evening at 7.30. He believes his life is a gift from the Mother.

Devotee 34: I have come here for a look/vision of the Goddess. It is just to have a look at Her. I am looking for blessings and goodwill. Let the Goddess keep my family well. The Goddess will definitely listen to me.

Devotee 35: The Goddess is worshipped in different manners by different people. Some light a lamp. Some ring the temple bells and savour the resounding harmony from it.

Devotee 36: She is sometimes our mother, sometimes our father—She is everything to us.

Devotee 37: There are always ups and downs in life. I have become a pauper, but have not collapsed—I will remain standing.

Devotee 38: This is a place of absolute faith. It is like the sloka says—there are various forms of worship. The kind of thought and faith you come with you will get back from this place.

Devotee 39: When we sit here at night and look at Her, throughout the evening, between 2.00 and 3.00 in the morning, we see devotees come—like clouds from the north that seem to envelop the Mother—and then they disappear.

Devotee 40: The meaning of a temple is where the mind and the heart merge.

Devotee 41: Mother says whatever we want She will give; in whatever manner we call Her, She will come to us.

Juhi Chawla: It is not just the Kamakhya Temple but the entire area surrounding the Kamrup region that is affected by the Mother's greatness and blessings. Everything has its existence from here. Unwavering faith in the Mother is the only objective.

2

SOMNATH TEMPLE

A mighty structure overlooking the Arabian Sea, which is not just a symbol of faith but a historical, religious and cultural beacon that has stood the test of time, is the Somnath Temple. Located in Saurashtra, Gujarat, and believed to have been created out of gold by the moon god Som, it is regarded as the first among the twelve Jyotirlinga shrines of Shiva.

Juhi Chawla: When there was nothing, He was omnipresent. When there will be utter emptiness, He will still be there. For aeons, people have an ingrained belief that there is a mystical power that has tied together so many millions of people. Sometimes with hands raised in faith and sometimes with hands folded in obeisance; sometimes carrying thalis of holy offerings, and at others bearing the holy books in faith—through these, all of us are engaged in a continual search for Him.

I, Juhi Chawla, will take you on such a sojourn, which is a unification of all such feelings, which traverses thousands of miles and draws people to the places where we may find

Him. The experience of that faith, this journey, is of the conviction that we will.

The area has a devotional feel and fervour—there are floral offerings, chantings and natural beauty all around.

A lady expressing her belief in faith: Sometimes one tires of the journey of life—that we are not getting what we seek, or what we want done our way is just not happening. If we can concentrate on the Almighty, on Omkar, on Mrityunjoy (One Who Conquers Death), all these problems will get resolved. When it is such, it feels as though God is with us, and we will be helped in emerging from our problems.

Juhi Chawla: When we bow in obeisance at the threshold, He embraces us. It is He who has drawn me to Him.

Devotee 1: Shivji, Brahma, Vishnu and Maheshwar can be seen here.

Devotee 2: You must have heard that during the era of Ram, when Lord Ram vanquished Tarakasur the demon, even after that, he respectfully touched his feet. Lakshman then asked: why are you showing him so much respect? The answer was that it is not him that I am saluting but the Divinity that lies within him.

Devotee 3: At one point I had no food to eat and no money either. Then with utter devotion I prayed to Shiva and said: O Almighty, please look at me. Then He looked in my direction and everything was sorted, and even my work started faring well. He is Time incarnate.

Devotee 4 (young man): My life and business are entirely due to the blessings of Shiva. That is why I have named my institution 'Shivam'.

Devotee 5 (lady with a child): One of my children is in the Army and posted in Srinagar. With the blessings of the Lord, he has marched ahead to protect everyone.

Juhi Chawla: In Gujarat, about 200 km from Rajkot, is situated Prabhas Patan. It is proof of the undying belief and emblem of a die-hard belief. Here is the permanent place of the universally renowned self-manifesting Shiva linga, Somnath. The holiest of holy pilgrim centres of India, this divine shelter is redolent of divinity. This is the place where the flames of devotion, faith and belief are lit in the hearts of millions.

Devotee 6: The desire of every devotee who comes to the Somnath Temple, no matter what it is, is fulfilled.

Devotee 7: I have been coming to the Somnath Temple since I was a child. Lord Shiva is our family deity. We have been worshipping Him for four generations.

Devotee 8: I have come from Bihar.

Devotee 9: I have come from Madhya Pradesh.

Devotee 10: I have come from Jabalpur.

Devotee 11: I have come from Nepal.

Devotee 12: Every time I come here, I am rejuvenated for a month. And whenever I feel the need again, I return and my energy is restored.

Devotee 13: This is truly a temple where one gets peace.

Devotee 14: The peace that I have not got from either my profession, my business or technology, I have amply got from the Lord in this temple.

Sage: Come here, worship and go away feeling recharged.

Juhi Chawla: The holy grounds of Somnath have been blessed by the mystical and the divine. This land is believed to be part of Prabhash Kshetra. 'Prabash', in other words, means light or enlightenment.

Parag Jayendra Pathak (priest of the temple trust): Just like there is no other pilgrim centre facing the vast ocean, similarly in this universe, too, there is nothing as vast and sprawling as this sprawling Earth. This is replete with the divine aura of Shiva. This is Prabhash Kshetra.

Devotee 15: Prabhash Kshetra is also known as Harihar Kshetra. This is because about 3 km from here, there is a sthanak, meaning station or stoppage; this is where Sri Krishna completed all that He had come on Earth to accomplish, and had departed for swargagaman, or left for the heavens. So this locale is believed to be holy as it is.

Parag Jayendra Pathak: Since Prabhash is a strong pilgrim centre, Somnath was manifested here.

Juhi Chawla: History says that innumerable devotees of Shiva have actually caught glimpses of Bholenath (Shiva) here. This still holds true. Many come to worship the Shiva linga in the hope of getting Lord Shiva's blessings.

Devotee 16: There are innumerable Shiva lingas all over India, but the first to be found was at Somnath.

Devotee 17: This is the first of the twelve Jyotirlingas.

Priest: In order to take form on Earth, Lord Shiva took the form of a linga. Any part where Shiva left any token of his body took the form of a Shiva linga.

Juhi Chawla: The greatness of Shiva shows the way and magnetically draws devotees to Him, illuminating their lives. It is believed that the sanctified Jyotirlingas are in sixty-four places, where the presence of Lord Shiva is felt. Of them, twelve are accepted as the holiest, and it is proven that Somnath is the last resting place of Shiva.

Priest: There are five elements: Earth, Water, Fire, Air and the Firmament. Then in our bodies, there are four elements: Mana, Buddhi, Chitta and Ego. When there is a mingling of the male and the female, a third being is born. The five and the four make up nine; and male, female and being (jeev), these three make up twelve Jyotirlingas.

Juhi Chawla: The twelve Jyotirlingas have been named after those true devotees of Shiva who have truly worshipped him. Shiva Himself has chosen these places as his abode. There, Shiva, in his own form, is worshipped with love and devotion.

Devotee 18: This Jyotirlinga is made of two elements—Som, meaning the Moon, and Nath, which is Shiva.

Devotee 19: Thousands of people have had their wishes fulfilled in Somnath, which is why so many people pay their obeisance there.

Devotee 20: We had prayed for our own house and it was fulfilled.

Devotee 21: I had fasted and also prayed to the Lord that I get married to the man I love, and now, I also have a baby.

Devotee 22: I started a small business in a village, and now, I also have a wholesale depot. Bholenath has showered on me much more than I deserve.

Juhi Chawla: Shiva fulfils the desires of all those who come to Him seeking His kindness. There is freedom from all sins. That is why He is also known as Bholenath. The piety and kindness of Shiva lies not only in the heart of His devotees, but also resounds in the celestial heavens.

According to the Puranas, Lord Brahma's son Dakshya Prajapati had twenty-seven daughters, who are known as the twenty-seven constellations.

All of them were married to Chandra. He behaved well with Rohini but not with the others. So the twenty-six daughters went to their father and said they were not treated well. Dakshyaraj tried to talk to Chandra, but he started laughing sardonically. This angered Dakshyaraj, who cursed Him with a debilitating medical condition. All the medicines on earth began losing their lustre because it is the Moon that turns medicines into nectar. Chandra went to Brahma and was told to go to Prabhash Bhumi, and worship Lord Shiva there.

Devotee 23: There, he worshipped Shiva (Shankar).

Juhi Chawla: Shiva then appeared in all His glory and Chandra was released from the curse inflicted on Him.

Devotee 24: Shivji granted Chandra a place on His forehead.

Devotee 25: He blessed the Moon by saying that for fifteen days, he would be illuminated, but for the rest of the fifteen days there would be darkness. The Moon requested one more boon—that just as His blessing had lifted his curse, let Him destroy all suffering in the universe and take up residence here in the form of a phallic stone, or a linga.

Juhi Chawla: Shiva accepted, and in the form of a Jyotirlinga became the Nath (Lord) of Somdev and remained here for all time; Somnath is symbolic of faith and devotion.

Devotee 26: If you worship the Shiva linga with true devotion, a magical aura can be felt.

Devotee 27: There is greater faith that God is here.

Devotee couple: One constantly feels like looking at the Somnath linga, and keep standing there.

Devotee couple 2: The atmosphere is so pure that one feels like being here for hours.

Juhi Chawla: Lord Somnath is worshipped three times a day. Prior to this, Lord Shiva's ablutions are done with Panchamrit (Panchamrut), meaning five nectars, and special holy ingredients.

When the conch shell and musical instruments are sounded before Shiva, it is as though all hopes and desires prostrate themselves before Him. The resounding of 'Om' stills the disturbed mind. For a short while, all senses become immersed in Shiva.

Devotee couple 3: I have come here three or four times. At the time of worship, I have circled the shrine four times and been able to see and worship Shiva.

Juhi Chawla: At Somnath, thanks to even a glimpse of Shiva, waves of hope rise in the heart. The consecrated holy food offered with devotion and dedication turns into the holy food of belief and the mind is sanctified by divine blessings.

The history of the Somnath Temple is one of honour and pride. To protect its honour many wars and battles have been waged and many people have sacrificed their lives for this.

Devotee 28: In these grounds of Prabhash Kshetra, this temple of Shiva is believed to have been broken sixteen times. There is reference in the Puranas that Lord Rama also had the Somnath Temple built; so did Krishna; so did the Tirthankaras of the Jains; and so did Ravana.

Juhi Chawla: The Prabhas Patan Museum, consisting of rare collections, stones and metals, are proof of the inner riches and treasures of the temple. Birth, death and creation, and happiness, sorrow and peace are forms of maya, or illusion. To find a release from this illusion, thousands of devotees reach the Triveni Sangam.

Devotee 29: About 1 km from here is believed to be the Triveni Sangam, of the Hiranya, the Saraswati and the Kapila. If you bathe in this confluence, or sangam, all sins are washed away. It is believed to be a very special place to offer obsequies to our ancestors.

This is because after the battle of the Mahabharata, when Arjuna expressed his sorrow to Lord Krishna, He responded by saying, 'If you feel this way, go to Prabhash Kshetra and offer all obsequies there for the Kauravas.' Ever since, the ritual of obsequies has been observed there.

Juhi Chawla: Here, the norm is of offering rituals. A certain type of dough, which is dedicated to of our ancestors, is immersed in the confluence of the three rivers and thus blessings are showered on the devotees. In turn, the devotees are released from their earthly ties and bonds.

Just as a river flows and merges into the ocean, the human soul becomes one with the Ultimate Being through this offering and is blessed with moksha—the ultimate release. That is why people come here from near and far to offer obsequies at this hallowed Triveni.

If you take even a step here, your ancestors laugh in joy because what they want, what they are looking for, they get it all.

If you look in the southern direction, towards the ocean, there is a pillar that also supports a placard. It has been said that Yama (the God of Death) and pitaron (forefathers) are situated in the south. So, from this sanctified Yamlok there is believed to be a direct path to Prabhash Kshetra; there is no obstruction.

There is a merging of the river with the ocean here. The oceans merge with the gods, and the gods become one with this land. This is the land of Harihar, Prabhash Kshetra.

Lighting the lamp of devotion in their hearts, millions of devotees visit Somnath every day. But the sight during Mahashivaratri is indeed indescribable. The devotees' desire is to anoint Bholenath with tokens of their devotion, and in order to catch a glimpse of him, devotees from all over the world gather here, and the majestic and colourful ceremony is enjoyed with fervour.

Devotee 30: Just as humans celebrate their birthday once a year, this is the one day of the Lord, and everything is done at home. This is a special place.

Devotee 31: On Shivaratri, Shiva celebrated his marriage to Parvati and by ingesting poison, He came to be known as 'Neelkanth', the One with the Blue Throat.

Priest: The outstanding feature of Mahashivaratri is that during the New Moon, the baser qualities of man come to the fore; and the lord of these qualities is Lord Shiva. On the day of Shivaratri, if one constantly prays to Shiva, these baser effects do not cause any harm.

If Shiva is worshipped in this manner, sins accumulated in successive births are nullified. If Shiva is worshipped and some special prayer is offered to him, there is no doubt that the prayers will be granted.

Someone from a group of young girls: My mother was not well at all, and we came here to pray that she recovers, and she did! That is why now every year we come here to offer prayers.

Juhi Chawla: At Somnath, the pennant of love flutters high at the peak of faith, where waves of thoughts sing melodies of devotion. When there is the sunrise of faith, the darkness of faithlessness melts away. Just as Shiva destroyed the perils of Somdev, or Chandra, similarly the hazards of his devotees are done away with by the Somnath Jyotirlinga carved in stone, this image of Bholenath, this Bholenath.

3

GOLDEN TEMPLE

Divinity dwells in the arms of peace and we know this for certain when in the sacred lands of Amritsar. Within the peaceful and blissful premises of the Harmandir Sahib Gurudwara in Amritsar, also widely known as the Golden Temple, devotees have claimed to find the real meaning of the Greater Being. The continuous chant from the verses of the Guru Granth Sahib adds to the sanctified atmosphere. The focus of the Golden Temple is the famous Amrit Sarovar, a water tank that surrounds the shrine. The sacred water from this holy pool of nectar is known for its healing powers.

Juhi Chawla: When there was nothing, He was omnipresent. When there will be utter emptiness, He will still be there. For aeons, people have an ingrained belief that there is a mystical power that has tied together so many millions of people. Sometimes with hands raised in faith and sometimes with hands folded in obeisance; sometimes carrying thalis of holy offerings, and at others bearing the holy books in

faith—through these, all of us are engaged in a continual search for Him.

I, Juhi Chawla, will take you on such a sojourn, which is a unification of all such feelings, which traverses thousands of miles and draws people to the places where we may find Him. The experience of that faith, this journey, is of the conviction that we will.

The fundamental element of the Sikh religion is the soul Omkar, which basically means 'God is One'. He is the One who is omnipresent. It is like the sweetest melody, which resounds in Him, to those who seek shelter in the Guru or the Ultimate Spiritual Mentor.

Devotee 1: I am from Jharkhand.

Devotee 2: I am from West Bengal.

Devotee 3: In 2005, I had come here for the first time. Since then, I have been coming here every two months.

Devotee 4: If after every six months or a year we do not come here, there is a strange kind of restlessness in us, telling us we must pay a visit.

Devotee 5: We have been here for the past four days, and we just do not feel like going back.

Devotee 6: There is a great feeling of relaxation here.

Devotee 7: The entire day we spend here—we just don't feel like going anywhere else.

Devotee 8: It is not just Indians, there are also a lot of overseas visitors here.

Juhi Chawla: The soul is satiated here. Amritsar, the religious capital of Punjab, is situated about 230 km from Chandigarh, the political capital of Punjab. Here is situated one of the most frequented pilgrim centres—Sri Harmandir Sahib.

Devotee 9: No sooner do you enter the gate than all your mental burdens just vanish. A man loses all his worries.

Devotee 10: There is so much peace after coming here. The soul finds peace and one forgets everything except the eternal.

Devotee 11: When I sit here, all tensions are forgotten and there is peace. Even if we just sit here, it feels like we are worshipping.

Devotee 12: What we cannot tell anyone we can communicate directly to God here.

Devotee 13: If anyone has any sorrow, problem or pain, Baba takes care of it all.

Juhi Chawla: Harmandir Sahib is renowned the world over as the Golden Temple. This is one of the holiest places in the world, where people of all religion, caste and creed congregate to worship.

Davinder Singh, Protocol Officer, Sri Harmandir Sahib: To the Sikh religion, the Golden Temple is regarded as the pinnacle of piety. It is believed that the Sikhs consider the Golden Temple to be the holiest place, but I believe this is supreme for all people in the world, as the message we get here is the message of humanity.

A foreign national: The first time I had contact with a Sikh was when I was walking in the desert, and a Sikh man gave me a lift. He was one of the most kind and gentle souls I have ever met. He paid for my food and everything else I needed and basically brought me back to life. He showed me what it meant to be a true man.

Devotee 14: Six months back I had made up my mind to stop shaving and present myself as a Sikh at Amritsar; only then will my life be fulfilled.

Juhi Chawla: The boundaries of Harmandir Sahib are sprawling, consisting of innumerable gigantic structures; it is a palace in itself. Some examples are the Akal Takht, the museum and the various places to stay in. Immediately on going in from the main entrance, there is a moat. Devotees wash their feet here and then ascend the marble stairs. It feels as though they have entered another world altogether. There is a large water reservoir here—the Amrit Sarovar. At the centre of this is the Harmandir Sahib. The fourth Guru of the Sikhs, Guru Ramdas, was responsible for the construction of the Golden Temple. In 1587, the fifth Guru, Guru Arjan Dev, completed the project. Right at the centre of this project is a darbar, or a kind of conference hall, which has been named Darbar Saham ('Saham' means God).

Devotee 15: No matter what the belief or who the follower, everyone is welcome here.

Devotee 16 (young girl): Everybody is treated the same here.

Devotee 17: There are four entrances here, and everyone, whether Hindu, Muslim, Sikh or Jew, is free to enter.

Devotee 18: Everyone is welcome here—enter, worship and feel fulfilled.

Devotee 19: I have a lot of faith in the Gurudwara, and the faith here is so strong that it is impossible to put all my thoughts into words.

Devotee 20: When visitors come here, they get a lot of peace. For all of them, it is a matter of reverence.

Devotee 21: Just like Muslims go to Mecca and Medina, for us it is very important that we visit the Golden Temple at least once in our lives.

Juhi Chawla: No matter what the religion, what the religious mentors say is all the same—that in this universe all of us are the same. In all of us, the enlightening force of the gurus is all the same. The Guru Granth Sahib is the supreme guide.

One can find in the Guru Granth Sahib our history and lineage. After our gurus this is what has been left behind for us, to help us move forward and take the Sikh religion forward.

Sage: After Guru Gobind Singh, the tenth Guru of the Sikhs, came to realize that in the future all those who come will declare themselves self-gurus, he understood that this would bring about a lot of problems, because everyone would turn into a spiritual mentor. So he allowed the flames of his spiritual prowess to be vested in the Guru Granth Sahib.

He created the holy book and put in the words of all the Gurus there; and he instructed all Sikhs to accept this as the Ultimate Guru and not any other, so there is no one to misguide anyone. Everything is stated clearly in the Guru Granth Sahib.

Davinder Singh: The tenth Guru bowed before the book he created and offered ₹5 and a coconut, vesting it with the status of the 'Ultimate Guru', which is now referred as the 'Sri Guru Granth Sahib'.

Temple official: When Guruji named the Guru Granth Sahib the Ultimate Guru, there must have been some sort of thought or logic behind it. A human being can make a mistake, but it is impossible for him to do so.

The Guru Granth Sahib is the embodiment of all ten previous Gurus. It's the truth. When you read it at specific times, it has powerful insights. Beautiful!

Juhi Chawla: Harmandir Sahib is regarded as the heart of Amritsar. Amritsar took its name from Amritsarovar, which the fourth Guru of the Sikhs, Guru Ramdas, made with his own hands. The waters of this sarovar are regarded as having the qualities of nectar. That is why the name of this city came to be Amritsar.

By bathing in nectar-like waters, one can wash away all sorrows and sins of this life. That is the reality.

A foreign tourist: There are so many people who have offered their prayers in the water here; there are so many mantras always being spoken here that the water vibrates at a very high spiritual frequency. And so it has healing properties.

Juhi Chawla: On one side of the Amritsarovar there is a plum tree. This has been regarded as one that can take away all sorrow. The story of this tree is a very touching and emotional one.

It is believed that in the nearby Patti village, there was a wealthy zamindar, or landowner. He had five talented and beautiful daughters. The Patti ka Badshah asked his daughters: who is responsible for feeding you? All answered that he was the one responsible. But one of his daughters was devoted to God and answered that it was God who fed her. She was punished and married off to a leper. One day as they were on their way to a pilgrimage, she left him at a spot near the gurudwara and went to find food for her husband and herself. Her husband noticed that the black crows that plunged into the Amritsarovar turned into swans. Somehow and with a great deal of effort he plunged in too, and all his illness was cured. When his wife returned, she could not recognize her husband and started searching for him. Her husband said that he was the same person she had left behind. She was amazed and asked how that was possible, since she had taken him to so many pilgrimage centres but nothing of the sort had ever happened.

Devotee 22: The wrist with which he had held on to the side of the lake was still uncured, and when he dipped it, it, too, was cured. That is how all sorrows are done away with. People come here to take a dip and it is believed that if done with full faith, no matter what the illness, it gets completely cured.

This is not just a story, but has also happened with me. I had broken out in rashes. Even I got cured at the Amritsarovar, and now, without having taken any medicines, there is not even a mark left.

Devotee 23: A friend of my nephew had his chest covered in boils, which were just not getting cured, and even his face had begun to get affected. You won't believe this, but he bathed in the Amritsarovar just once and when he came to me after ten days, he had been cured.

Devotee 24: A girl had come to Amritsar from Kapurthala. Doctors told her that she would never be able to see again, but her eyes got cured at the Golden Temple. Even her ears, which had stopped working, were cured. That girl still lives in Kapurthala and is now perfectly all right.

A female devotee: A man had cancer and the doctors had given up all hope. The doctors had said that he would not survive. People suggested that he come here and serve the temple. That is what he did and now he is perfectly all right, and the doctors are stunned. This is the truth.

Juhi Chawla: A very important part of the Sikh religion is service. This is a truly religious concept, which says that every Sikh should spend time according to his capability and capacity in helping those in need. In the Guru Granth Sahib, service has been given a very important place. This inspires all Sikhs to offer their services to society without any ulterior motive. The feeling of service not only propagates the feeling of brotherhood among men but also sows the seeds of positivity in their minds.

Devotee 25: I have great faith in the Sikh religion. The people of this religion have a humility and feeling of service that I have never seen elsewhere.

Devotee 26: There are many highly placed Sikh people who are seen serving. They do the kind of work that no one else does.

Devotee 27: Here, service of devotees continues all the time. All those who love and come here to serve with a clean mind will receive blessings in abundance.

Devotee 28: True service is what is done with the mind. It's like the feeling when you are content with the food that you have eaten—it cannot be put into words. That is the kind of feeling, and it is different from anything else. When physical service is offered with a clean mind, the mind is purified and any kind of illness is vanquished.

Devotee 29: The best of all work is service. It is after a very long time that men get a chance to engage in the act of service.

Devotee 30: When you serve, you really feel very good. It is not something that can be expressed.

Juhi Chawla: Let welfare be bestowed upon all. It is by following this principle that the Sikh religion has prospered. The proof of this is the Guru ka Langar. It will not be wrong to say that Guru ka Langar is another form of serving the Guru. All men are the same and there is the divine in everybody. All are welcome at Harmandir Sahib.

Whether one is rich or poor makes no difference. You are welcome and the same blessed food is prepared in the same manner for everybody. The system is the same for everything.

My daughter had come with me, and yesterday even she did her part of service. Nobody asked, 'What religion do you follow?' Rather, 'If you want to serve, take your seat and serve as much as you will. Here, there are zero differences between religions and no scope for any kind of discord. It is a place of God and everybody is welcome here.'

The story goes that the system of langar was begun by the first Guru, Guru Nanak. His father had given him ₹20 and told him to do some honest business with it. So he used the money to feed hungry sages. That tradition continued to grow and has become what it is today. From that langar worth ₹20 it has spread to millions.

Everybody is seated together and has their meals together, and this food is regarded as blessed food.

We eat food and it goes to the stomach. But when the food comes from here, it is blessed and the value increases so much that it cannot be expressed. No matter how you make the same puris and vegetables at home, the taste will never be the same as at a langar.

The peace that one gets after praying at the Harmandir Sahib remains etched in one's memories forever. It remains as a blessing in our lives. At night when the Palki Sahib procession emerges, it is impossible to describe the sight in words. Amid the holy chanting of 'Sat Naam Vahe Guru', when the Guru Granth Sahib, covered in coloured cloth is carried on the shoulders of the bearers and moves towards the Akal Takht for rest, such a mystical and holy ambience is created! The minds, hearts and bodies of everyone participating are focused solely on the procession.

Devotee 31: For anyone who has seen the palanquin of Guru Granth Sahib, it has been nothing short of amazing. You get goosebumps.

Juhi Chawla: It is believed that if one has to feel eternity, he/she has to visit Harmandir Sahib at least once in their lives. It is not wrongly said that if, keeping the mind clean, one can prostrate oneself at the feet of the True Lord, feeling His magnificence and partaking of His blessed food, one will never return empty-handed.

Devotee 32: All my desires have been fulfilled here; I did not speak about them to anyone.

Devotee 33: My child's father passed away, but I unburdened my sorrows to God and He rectified everything.

Devotee 34: Whatever I have wanted He has given.

Devotee 35: Where there is belief and where there is truth, the Almighty will be found and everything will be good; nothing untoward can happen there.

4

GANPATIPULE

Along the beautiful Konkan coastline of Maharashtra is the quaint hamlet of Ganpatipule—the abode, according to popular belief, of a self-manifested idol of Lord Ganesha. Worshipped as the eternal guardian of the entire western region of India, the Ganesha idol here is said to be about 400 years old. Thousands of devotees who throng the Ganpatipule Temple every year have one thing in common—the everlasting faith that even a small glimpse of their beloved Lord Ganpati can bring them peace and happiness. With the sound of waves that calms your soul and serenity that surrounds your being, the Ganpatipule Temple is sure to connect you with the divine.

Juhi Chawla: When there was nothing, He was omnipresent. When there will be utter emptiness, He will still be there. For aeons, people have an ingrained belief that there is a mystical power that has tied together so many millions of people. Sometimes with hands raised in faith and sometimes with hands folded in obeisance; sometimes carrying thalis of holy offerings, and at others bearing the holy books in faith—through these, all of us are engaged in a continual search for Him.

I, Juhi Chawla, will take you on such a sojourn, which is a unification of all such feelings, which traverses thousands of miles and draws people to the places where we may find Him. The experience of that faith, this journey, is of the conviction that we will.

In the vicinity of Ratnagiri, near the coastal region, in that beautiful and holy place, is established the deity of Sri Ganeshji.

Devotee 1: Whenever we go to any temple, to look up on the visage of God, automatically we feel a sense of serenity. God is right behind us and whatever we do, it will definitely be good. We look up on Him as 'Vighnaharta'—the destroyer of all impediments. Anything that troubles us will be turned away. That is why we like coming here.

Devotee 2: When we go to meet God, there is a different kind of peace. I seem to draw energy for the entire year when I come here.

Devotee 3: The heart overflows with feelings of devotion for Ganpati. It becomes difficult to say anything. This 'darshan', or the sight of God, I carry home with me, waiting to return next year. When we enter, and, after taking a look, we sit down for two minutes, the peace and serenity is like nowhere else. That is why I like coming back here.

Devotee 4: There is a sheer sensation that God is here.

Devotee 5: There is a clear feeling of joy.

Devotee 6: Coming there, there is no need to ask for anything—we come in love and go in love.

Devotee 7: There is such strength in nature that we are always called. He is definitely around us. There is always a feeling that 'if you do good, only good will happen with you'. Never waver—even if you are alone, it does not matter. He is always with you. It is faith in God that takes us forward, and what is faith is strength.

Juhi Chawla: At a distance of 340 km from Mumbai is the Ratnagiri district. This beautiful village is renowned for the splendour of the Konkan coast. In the indescribable beauty of this coastal town, near the sandy shores, is located the Ganpatipule Mandir. This temple, situated near the shore, is very old. The natural beauty here is of a different kind altogether, and cannot be seen everywhere.

Devotee 8: There is absolute peace here, and it is as though my batteries are recharged by the time I leave.

Devotee 9: Here you will only find devotion; and it is because of this devotion that people come here. I have full faith in Him and depend completely on Him. That is why we do whatever is needed to come here.

Devotee 10: I have come from Kolhapur, and have been coming here since I was five years old, since 1973.

Devotee 11: I am forty-nine years old and have come here at least a hundred times.

Devotee 12: I have been coming here since I was eight years old. There was nothing here but the temple structure then.

Juhi Chawla: There have been a lot of changes in the upkeep of the temple. But the undying devotion to Bappa (Ganesh), which has been flowing ceaselessly for the past 400 years, remains the same.

The name Ganpatipule is linked with Ganeshji. In front lies the seashore full of sand—sand is known as 'valu' in Marathi and 'pulan' in Sanskrit. Ganeshji sits on a throne on the pulan, hence the name Ganpatipule.

This self-created image is also known as Lambodara. This is the name He is known by. Nobody has placed or constructed it here.

According to the Mudgal Purana, for the security of the land known as India, and her people, eight temples of Ganpati were established in eight directions. The fifth was established in Ganpatipule, which is the protector of the western side; it is Vakratunda in Madras, Mahodar in Rameswar, Gajanan in Tanjavar, Ekdanta in Kaldi, Kerala, Vikat in Kashmir, Vighnaraja in the Himalayas, and Dhumravat in Tibet. He ensures protection in each direction.

In the face of the destroyer of all problems, Vighnaharta Ganesha helps devotees give up all their worries. There is an unshakeable belief that each and every devotee is given the same place in His heart as everyone else.

Devotee 13: Ganpati is our own. He is like a family member with whom we can share everything.

Devotee 14: He has been looking after us since our childhood, and He will be my protector till my death. What else do I need in life? I don't ask for anything from Him—as a matter of fact, I only ask forgiveness from Him.

Devotee 15: If I see Him, there is joy. There is only joy there, and nothing else.

Devotee 16: Just as we look into the eyes of a person when we speak, when we look into His eyes, we seem get everything we want.

Devotee 17: When we look up Him, a kind of aura engulfs us.

Devotee 18: I don't know what, but there is something special in this image. He seems to be the closest to any of us.

Juhi Chawla: In Ganpatipule, He has sprung into being straight from the lap of nature itself. He has been known for just 400 years, but in a strange and mystical fashion, He has been presiding here for all eternity.

There was a headman here by the name of Bhriguji and he was a devotee of Ganeshji. One night, he had a dream that Ganeshji had come to his village and that he should find Him. Bhriguji had a cow that would be milked in the courtyard. But she would usually yield more milk if she were taken to graze on the mountainside—but that had stopped happening. It occurred to the headman that someone was stealing the milk. He told the herdsman who looked after the cow to keep an eye on her. The herdsman saw that when the cow had finished grazing, she would go to a place (Ganpatipule) and yield milk at a spot all on her own. The herdsman cleaned the area and from there emerged the stone that is now revered as Ganpati. And the stone is considered wish-fulfilling.

People have as much faith in Him as in the depths of the immeasurable ocean. They have the firm belief that in any prayers to Ganeshji, there is a certain magic. That Ganeshji can take care of any problem or sorrow.

Devotee 19: Ganeshji can ingest all kinds of sorrows and problems. That is why he is known as Lambodara.

Devotee 20: Ever since I was born, I have believed in Ganeshji. He means the world to me. If there is any worry or problem, just chanting His name can solve all of them. It's true.

Devotee 21: I had asked for a child when we had come to visit Ganapati. I got His blessing and now I have a child— that, too, within a year.

Devotee 22: I am sure that everyone will be going back with His blessings. After all, He is Vighnaharta, or the One who can destroy all problems. Nothing bad can happen if you have faith in Him.

Devotee 23: Whenever bad times fall upon us, we pray to Ganesha. We send up to Him in prayers all the desires that we have in our heart, and He shows us the path to decimate these dangers. That is how we do away with our problems and sorrows, and remain healthy.

Devotee 24: For thirty-six years I have been serving Ganpatiji. For the past three–four years, there has been some pain in my legs, but, even then, I have never stopped serving Him. The pain in my legs gradually stopped and I could serve Him again properly.

Devotee 25: Today I have no illness or disease. There is complete relaxation. I have been on a fast since morning. I have not even had water so far, but I am full of energy, thanks to the powers of Ganpatipule.

Juhi Chawla: How a devotee prays depends on the problems he/she has. Then the Lord appears to them in the desired form. That is why devotees come to Ganpatipule for a sight of Ganpati Bappa. If anyone has lost sight of the true path, then Vakratunda points out the right direction to them, and if someone is looking for peace, then He appears as Mangalmurti.

Devotee 26: During times of difficulty, we are reminded of Ganapati. That's it, once we have said our prayers, there will be no more problems.

Devotee 27: Though his eyes are small, they see a lot; with his large ears he is able to hear everything.

Devotee 28: God is imbued with all kinds of qualities. If His positive elements are transmuted to us by even .001 per cent, our birth as a human will have been worthwhile.

Devotee 29: Shree and Om are very important elements in religion. The universe starts with Shree; and the universe is enmeshed in Om. This is our much-worshipped God of Maharashtra.

Juhi Chawla: The meaning of the Ganpati Upanishad, the existence of Ganesha, dates back to before the advent of Man and Nature (Purush and Prakriti). He is the One to take on any problem; is highly intelligent and an expert in the sixty-four arts; and his illimitable and undying love for His parents makes Him the best of all.

It is believed that once, Ganesha and his brother Kartikeya had a competition about who could go around the universe first. So Kartikeya set off on his stead, the peacock. But Ganesha clambered on to his, the mouse, and went right around both his parents and thus quickly completed his tour of the universe. He made it clear that his parents were his entire universe.

Shiva was pleased at this devotion and blessed Ganesha with the boon that he would always be the first to be worshipped whenever any kind of ceremony took place. Ever since, before the worship of any god, it is Ganesha who is worshipped first.

Devotee 30: If there is anything good that you want done, whether it is wedding or the starting of a new business, Ganpati is always worshipped first—all devotion is shown to Him first. In our family, during a wedding, a frame of Ganpati is hung above the door.

Devotee 31: The first right of any worship belongs to Ganpati. It is very auspicious that the year begins with worshipping Him.

Juhi Chawla: 'Aarti' is the outward worship or manifestation of that which leads us along the path of love for the Lord. To submit one's entire being at the feet of the Lord is what is known as 'aarti'.

Devotee 32: When we get a glimpse of Ganpati, there's nothing else in the mind but Him; there's complete focus on the image of Ganesha. Even if there is something that we think of wanting, at the actual time of seeing Him, all such thoughts vanish.

Devotee 33: It is only my task to touch his feet and show respect and devotion to Him—everything else is up to Him.

Devotee 34: Whatever comes to mind we tell Ganpatiji, and things start to automatically fall in place.

Devotee 35: Whatever is happening is happening because of His divine will. He gets us to do whatever is His will. Who are we to want to do anything? It is He who ensures that we do what He wants.

Devotee 36: Today is a very auspicious day—it is Ganesh Jayanti...

Devotee 37: You all have seen that Ganesh Chaturthi is celebrated in Mumbai. In Ratnagiri, it is not Ganesh Chaturthi but the birth of Ganesh that is celebrated.

Devotee 38: For the birth celebration of Ganeshji, it is essential for me to come here.

Juhi Chawla: Ganpati Jayanti, the day the devotees' favourite deity was born, is a day when their joy and jubilation of knows no limits. Throughout the day, arrangements are made for the blessed food to be cooked, including special sweetmeats and khichdi. On this day, another special ritual takes place. Ganpati Bappa is adorned and, with great care and love, taken in a palanquin for circumambulation around a hill, which is known as Ganpati's sub-form.

The small hillock that can be seen during the circumambulation is taken to be Ganpati's spot. Actually, the hillock itself is taken to be Ganpati. This is a sojourn of 1 kilometre.

Devotee 39: Now I am sixty-seven years old, but if I do not make this sojourn, there will be no joy for me. That is why what I have done today has brought me great joy.

Devotee 40: This is what we have experienced—our feet do not swell and there is no pain.

Devotee 41: By this we can show that we can never thank Him enough for all that He has done, but we can at least manifest our love and faith for Him through this.

Juhi Chawla: All devotees desire that the love and empathy of Bappa continue to be showered on them. They are alone with their Lord and can talk to Him about whatever is in their heart. They can beg for forgiveness for any sin and try to please Him in every manner.

Some sing or play musical instruments in front of Him, while others just think of Him from a distance. However, it seems to me that if one prays with all devotion and honesty, the prayers definitely reach Him and are granted.

Devotee 42: When we communicate with the Lord, it seems that no matter where we go, He is with us.

Devotee 43: We have come here entirely by chance, just wandering by. I have never prayed or worshipped as such. But I asked for something and it was fulfilled within six months. Everything changed for me and I started coming here often.

Devotee 44: Whatever I have was given by Him. There is nothing more that I want. My life is complete, I feel. Whatever life I have led so far has been by the grace of Ganesha.

Devotee 45: Whenever You are with me, there is no danger that can befall me. Whatever issues the future might hold will also be taken care of.

5

JWALAMUKHI MANDIR

Nestled in the lap of Kangra Ghat in Himachal Pradesh is the magical temple of Jwala Devi. Famous as one of the fifty-one Shakti peeths, the Jwala Devi Temple is unique as it does not have an idol placed inside, but just an eternal burning flame. Soft and serene, yet strong and intense, the flame represents a mother's love. Devotees thronging the temple staunchly believe that a glimpse of the burning flame shall lead to the end of their struggles and pave the way for happier days. Intricately woven tales, fascinating legends and miracles will take you on a spiritual journey in this chapter.

Juhi Chawla: When there was nothing, He was omnipresent. When there will be utter emptiness, He will still be there. For aeons, people have an ingrained belief that there is a mystical power that has tied together so many millions of people. Sometimes with hands raised in faith and sometimes with hands folded in obeisance; sometimes carrying thalis of holy offerings, and at others bearing the holy books in

faith—through these, all of us are engaged in a continual search for Him.

I, Juhi Chawla, will take you on such a sojourn, which is a unification of all such feelings, which traverses thousands of miles and draws people to the places where we may find Him. The experience of that faith, this journey, is of the conviction that we will.

Himachal Pradesh is an outstanding example of a divine region/place, which mesmerizes the mind. Divinity is in the very air of the state and is felt as a potent force in every corner. There is an age-old potency here that has the power to change the direction of life for every visitor. This is situated in the lap of the Shivalik mountains, in Kangra Ghat; and to the south of this beautiful range, at a distance of about 34 km is situated the Jwalamukhi Mandir.

Devotee 1: It is Her great kindness that we have been able to get here and pray to Her.

Devotee 2: The Mother rids us of all carnal desire, rage, attraction to worldly goods, greed and vanity—and calls us to pay obeisance at Her feet. There, we forget everything except the Mother. I had brought some food, which I offered to the Mother.

Devotee 3: I live in Ludhiana and there is a kind of restlessness in my mind. When I am here, I am perfectly all right. This is my home. I mean this does not seem like a temple to me, but my own home. It is like I have some link with it from a previous birth, the ties of which I am fulfilling now.

Devotee 4: There is such a magnetic attraction about this temple that we are pulled in its direction.

Sage: She is the one who looks after all, and is the Mother of all beings.

Devotee 5: My mother can barely get up and it pains her to get up, but she has still come all this way to the temple.

Devotee 6: We have all been coming here since childhood.

Devotee 7: I make an effort to come here at least twice a year.

Devotee 8 (man carrying his old mother): This is the third time she has come to this temple. She has come on the back of my uncle and my father too.

Devotee 9: My mother has come here 110 times so far.

Devotee 10: I have come here from Rajasthan.

Devotee 11: I am from Rampur.

Devotee 12: I have been coming here since I was born. My ancestors used to come from Pakistan to offer their prayers here.

Devotee 13: It feels very good and relaxing to come here.

Dr Ashok Pathania (temple trustee): The Jwalamukhi Mandir is one of the peeths or pilgrim centres of the country. The burning tongue of the Mother is present here. She emits fire from her mouth and the entire place is thus known as Jwalamukhi.

Juhi Chawla: The Jwalamukhi Temple of Devi Jwalamukhi makes one feel the presence of Ma Jwala. This unique and incomparable holy place is not meant merely for Jwalamukhi or the people of Himachal Pradesh, but for all of humanity as an undeniable source of power.

Devotee 14: The outstanding thing about this place is that whatever one prays for is granted.

Devotee 15: The last time we had come, the Mother showed us something so marvellous! It was impossible for us to get blessed food or prasad, but when we emerged from the temple, my wife found in her bag a packet of prasad. There is the belief that the Mother is with us. Believe in Her and She will do what is necessary.

Devotee 16: The doctors had given up all hope that I would live. Then a devotee told me about this place and I came on foot and carried back in my heart the divine flame. From then till now, I am surviving without any medicine and without any treatment. There is no problem that cannot be cured here. This is a miracle in an era where evil reigns.

Devotee 17: The Mother fulfils the desires and prayers of millions of people all over.

Juhi Chawla: There is a tradition followed at the Jwalamukhi Temple. Whoever has their prayers fulfilled has to prostrate themselves and move forward in that position till the Goddess is reached and prayers are offered to Her.

Temple authority: All devotees of the world, in order to fulfil their desires and to ask the Mother for something, come to Mata Sri Jwalamukhi. You will have seen some devotees prostrating themselves and crawling forward from the entrance for about 1 km. Their prayers had been answered by the Mother—that is why they were doing this.

Juhi Chawla: Here, devotion is present not only in the minds of the devotees, but, in fact, in the form of a flame that is lit. Here Jwala Devi is not present in the form of any statue or image, but in the form of a flame that never dies. This flame of the Goddess has been burning for centuries. This mystical flame is what is worshipped here.

An intrigued little boy who saw the flame: I have seen the fire inside that keeps burning and never goes out.

Another boy: We have come to see the flame here—it never goes out and burns continually.

Ateet Sharma (temple priest): Whether you go to the Murti or the Pindi room, here the Goddess is in Her original form— the akhand jyoti—where She burns eternally with no oil or clarified butter; the flame remains ignited all the time— twenty-four hours a day, twelve months a year, year after year.

Juhi Chawla: There is such devotion and faith in the Mother that, like some magnetically attracted soul, devotees are drawn to this flame.

Devotee 18: The day I do not come to the temple, there is a strange kind of restlessness in me. I feel as though I have done nothing at all, and have earned nothing.

Devotee 19: If I am tense due to some reason, I close my eyes and try to visualize the flame. If I can, then I know that everything will be fine.

Sage: The sight that we possess cannot see the Divine. But Ma Jwalamukhi virtually takes form in front of us.

Devotee 20: Mata is the greatest. She is the one who has lit the light. That is why there is light throughout the universe.

Juhi Chawla: The mysticism and strength that is felt here has such an effect on everybody that just on seeing the divine flame, the hearts of all seem to dance with joy, and they all sing together in unison, 'Jai Mata Di!'

The energy here is infectious and it is obvious in the way devotees wait for hours just to get a glimpse of the Mother.

Devotee 21: I have been waiting in line for almost two–two and a half hours, but it feels very good to think that I am going to Mata's temple.

Devotee 22: This is the fundamental truth. All these people that you see here waiting patiently in line, are doing so only because they will be able to catch a glimpse of the Goddess who will be able to put right all that is wrong.

Devotee 23: There is a lot of peace here and it is a very nice place.

Devotee 24: The peace and tranquillity one finds here I don't think one finds anywhere else.

Devotee 25: I don't think there is anywhere in the world where I get so much peace.

Juhi Chawla: Where Jwalaji is worshipped as the prime force, there are eight other flames that have been conjoined with the other forms of Mata. The trustee of the place informs us that in the natal chamber of the temple (the garbha griha), there are seven other flames, each bearing a different name.

Priest: The first flame is that of Chandi Ma, the second of Ma Hingalaj, the third of Ma Bindyabasini, the fourth, which is the main flame, is of Ma Mahakali, the fifth is of Ma Annapurna and, after that, there are two more— Ma Mahasaraswati and Ma Mahalakshmi. They remain ignited all the time without any sort of fuel.

Juhi Chawla: The Mother's devotees feel Her presence in every single corner here. Through various avatars, or incarnations of the Goddess, Her devotees seek Her filial blessings and obtain benedictions of Her strength.

Devotee 26: At 4.00 in the morning my husband suddenly began panting and jerking his legs. I didn't know what was happening. My sister had come from Chandigarh, and she said, 'Ma has come and is seated here and the trident is placed here, and She has placed Her foot on my leg. She is asking why you are blocking Her path here.' Then even my husband saw Her in a vision and I had to accept that the Mother was everywhere.

Devotee 27: Devotion can be felt but never seen. And devotion is felt only from the inner being.

Devotee 28: What is there to ask from Mother? She knows everything. She gives by Herself and there is no need to ask Her for anything.

Devotee 29: No matter in what you seek Her, She will be found. All the relations that I have are all with Her or from Her.

Juhi Chawla: Sometimes, an actual vision so bewilders us that we cannot regard it as anything other than a miracle, and if this miracle is taking place inside the temple of Jwala Devi, our faith and devotion increase manifold. There is a feeling of miracle. In Gorakh Dibbi, on the premises of the temple, there is an ancient tale from the Puranas centring on Gorakhnath. The trustee of the temple informs us the first of the Nath clan, Gorakhnathji, had prayed to Mata Rani here. And Mata Rani had Herself appeared before him. This is the flame that keeps burning here.

According to a tale from the Puranas, Mata Rani asked Gorakhnath to partake of 'Tamasic food'. He responded that he would partake of water and khichdi. Further, he requested permission from Mata to heat some water for the food. He then proceeded to fill two bowls with water and set out to seek alms. It is believed that it was this point that saw the beginning of the Kalyug or the Negative Era. Gorakhnathji left for his heavenly abode then and there. It is said that the bowls he had filled are still kept there. But the water poured in them is cold. Only when the Age of Truth returns, will life return and it will be possible to cook in them.

Bubbles can be seen in the water reservoir there, which is taken to be a token of Mataji's promise. It is believed that Mata Jwalamukhi is awaiting the return of Baba Gorakhnath.

The water is calm, but smoke emerges from it. When the priest dips his hand into the water and takes it out, fire can be seen.

There are numerous stories of the powers of Mata Jwalamukhi told by the locals here. Of all of them, the most mystical and romantic centres on the character of the Mughal badshah Akbar, who was a great devotee of Mata.

Temple trustee: There is the legend of Dhyanu Bhagat here. Dhyanu Bhagat was a resident of Uttar Pradesh. He was passing through Delhi when it came to the ears of

Akbar that a mighty warrior under the leadership of Dhyanu Bhagat was going to offer prayers to Mata Jwala. He then asked for the reason. The answer he got was that in the town of Jwalamukhi, Mata Jwala, with Her infinite powers, was appearing before Her devotees.

Akbar severed the head of Dhyanu Bhagat's horse as a challenge to Mataji. If the Goddess was able to re-attach the severed head of the horse, he would accept Her powers. Dhyanu Bhagat sat down in deep meditation, and in the end also severed his head and set it down before the Goddess. The Goddess was pleased and not only appeared before him but also brought both Dhyanu Bhagat and his horse back to life.

Devotee 30: Akbar accepted the power of the Goddess and constructed an umbrella of gold. However, he was proud that only he could do something like that, but his ego was shattered when the umbrella was thrown down.

Devotee 31: The ego that Akbar had was finally destroyed here.

Devotee 32: You can still see the fallen umbrella here. No scientist has been able to deduce which metal it has changed into from gold.

Devotee 33: People of all age groups come here with great enthusiasm. It feels very good.

Devotee 34 (old man): This seventy-two-year-old body is proof of the fact that Mata makes climbing these difficult mountains as easy as walking in the fields. This is truly a miracle but She gives me strength.

Devotee 35 (young girl): You can ask Her whatever comes

to mind. There is no concern about whether She will grant our wish; even if She does not, it is Her will. But there will never be any pain from Her.

Devotee 36: Whatever problems, pain or tension there is, we pray to Her and it goes away.

Devotee 37: We cannot say that gods and goddesses cannot be seen—we have to have eyes like Dhyanu Bhagat and Meera Bai to see God. If our intentions are pure and good, God is still definitely here.

Juhi Chawla: Of the five times that prayers are offered to the Goddess, the most special is the shavan (bedtime) aarti at 10.00 p.m. This is completed in two parts. The first (showing of lights) is done in the main temple. The next is done in the Seja Bhawan, or the bedroom, located on the temple premises. There, in accordance with tradition, Mata's bed is decorated. Devotees believe that it is at this time that the Goddess is the most attentive to all pleas, when She is in the deepest part of Her sleep.

Devotee 38: It's like we say when She goes to the bedroom, She does not sleep, but picks up Her register. When She is looking through Her register and you are sitting outside and praying, it is your prayer that will be heard first.

Juhi Chawla: The entire universe is brought close because of Her. In the heat of your flames, I have felt coolness and serenity. Fire is pure and a symbol of strength. The flame of Mata Jwalamukhi brings to us this realization. This fiery power, like devotion and reverence, is illimitable and without any boundaries.

6

TRIMBAKESWAR TEMPLE

Just a few minutes away from Nashik city in Maharashtra is the pious town of Trimbak, a place that finds mention in the powerful Maha Mritunjaya Mantra. Mystical, powerful and enigmatic, the Jyotirlinga here has three faces that symbolize Lord Brahma, Lord Vishnu and Lord Mahesh. Lush green mountains encircling the temple lend it a beatific atmosphere, and devotees come here seeking peace. The holiness and purity of Trimbakeswar shall surely make you experience faith and spirituality.

Juhi Chawla: When there was nothing, He was omnipresent. When there will be utter emptiness, He will still be there. For aeons, people have an ingrained belief that there is a mystical power that has tied together so many millions of people. Sometimes with hands raised in faith and sometimes with hands folded in obeisance; sometimes carrying thalis of holy offerings, and at others bearing the holy books in faith—through these, all of us are engaged in a continual search for Him.

I, Juhi Chawla, will take you on such a sojourn, which is a unification of all such feelings, which traverses thousands of miles and draws people to the places where we may find Him. The experience of that faith, this journey, is of the conviction that we will.

We worship the three-eyed Lord Shiva, the One who looks after the entire universe. Your compassion and pity is the sustenance of our lives. I bow in obeisance to my Bholenath, Lord Shiva. The devotion includes innate feelings of reverence. If there is devotion, then you have found God; if that is lacking, no amount of good deeds will be of any use.

Devotee 1: If you do not believe, then everything is false. So it is your choice. It is faith that matters.

Juhi Chawla: In Maharashtra, at a distance of about 25 km from the city of Nashik is situated a small town by the name of Trimbak. In this small town one can find one of the twelve Jyotirlingas of Lord Shiva—the Trimbakeswar Temple.

Devotee 2: We are from Jammu and Kashmir.

Devotee 3: I am from Karnataka.

Devotee 4: A lot of people come here with faith and devotion, and on hearing about their experiences, I, too, have come.

Devotee 5: Our hopes in life have never been fulfilled, so we have come to Bholenath, Who makes it all happen.

Devotee 6: In any danger or problem, we remain strongly devoted to Shivji. His blessings are always with us. That is why we emerge unscathed from every problem.

Satyapriya Shukla (a local): 'Tri' means 'three' and 'ambak' means 'eye'. Since Lord Shiva has three eyes, He is known as 'Trimbakeswar' here. The remarkable feature about this is that all the other Jyotirlingas have been made by someone or the other, but this Jyotirlinga has not been established by anyone. Ever since creation itself, it has reigned supreme here, self-sanctified.

Juhi Chawla: In all the other twelve Jyotirlingas, it is only Shiva who is worshipped. But here, on entering the inner sanctum, if scrutinized carefully, three phallic stones of about one inch each can be seen. These stones, the Tridev, are regarded as the incarnations of Brahma, Vishnu and Mahesh. Why is this feature only found here? No particular allusion to this is found anywhere else. But one factor is clear—here, devotees get the opportunity to worship the three deities.

Scholar/holy man: Brahma possesses the qualities of Sattva (light, bliss, goodness); Vishnu possesses the qualities of Rajas (passion, motion); and Shankar possesses the qualities of Tamas (inertia, darkness). Trilokinath is the possessor of all three qualities, and that is what we believe—that all three deities are present here. That is why the entire world gravitates to this place and leaves after taking the Urja (power, strength).

Juhi Chawla: It is believed that if you put all your faith in Him, and, casting aside any selfishness, if you truly pray to Him, He will to appear to you. Yes, His appearance may be different. Here in Trimbakeswar, when whatever desires and hopes expressed by the devotees have been fulfilled, they have always caught a glimpse of Him.

Devotee 7 (from a group of five women): All wishes that are made are fulfilled. There is a lot, truly a lot, of belief here.

Devotee 8: Prior to my daughter's wedding, we had prayed very hard that everything goes off well—and that wish was fulfilled.

Devotee 9 (young boy): Whatever is asked for in full faith is bound to be fulfilled.

Devotee 10 (young girl): What I believe is that merely wanting something does not work. We want to know where God is. That is why we continue to come here. We believe God is here.

Devotee 11: About ten or twelve years ago, there was a kind of flood here; there was water everywhere. But no water entered the temple. It cannot be anything but a miracle! Then, half an hour after that, the entire village was emptied of all water. To my mind, it was a great miracle. And not just for me, for the entire village.

Juhi Chawla: After walking for a while inside the city, the main entrance of the Trimbakeswar Temple comes into sight. It is an architectural masterpiece. In 1755, Nana Saheb Balaji Bajirao had started its construction. Nana Saheb was the Peshwa, or ruler, of the Maratha kingdom.

Situated at the highest peak of the Sahyadri range, in proximity to Brahmagiri and the Godavari River, the temple stands in black stone. One's faith shoots up at the sight of the temple and on hearing the folk tales and narratives surrounding it.

There is a story related to the Trimbakeswar Temple, but with a twist.

Sri Dixit (priest): Actually, the Brahmagiri Parvat is in the form of Shiva. In the Puranas, there is a story that when Sati Mata was burnt to a cinder in her father's yajna ceremony, she was born again as Parvati. Brahma and Vishnu decided that they would try to track down Shiva. So in search of Shiva, Brahma went upwards and Vishnu began tracking his footsteps. Despite trying with all their might, they could not understand where Shiva could be. Brahma did not like this at all—after all, he was the Creator! So he took recourse to a lie. But Shiva knew all about this lie and He cursed Him to turn into a mountain.

Juhi Chawla: When Brahma was cursed, He was ashamed of Himself, and in order to be free from the curse, He sat in meditation. This pleased Shiva and His anger turned to benediction. He told Brahma that henceforth, in that place, he would be known by Shiva's name. That is why Shiva is present here as the Brahmagiri Parvat. If, according to one tale, Shiva resides here as the Brahmagiri Parvat, there is also a very romantic tale behind the Jyotirlinga form of Shiva here.

Dixitji: Many thousands of years ago, Gautam Rishi resided here. He meditated and his entire life went on in this manner. At that time, a great drought hit the country. People realized that only if they went to Gautam Rishi would they get some sustenance.

Devotee 12 (elderly man): In the morning, Gautam Rishi would plant paddy and, in the evening, when it would ripen, he would thresh it. He would then cook it and distribute it as blessed food.

Devotee 13 (young boy): He would plant paddy here, and one day on seeing a cow stray into the field, Gautam Rishi went to chase him away. But the cow suddenly died. Then all the rishis gathered and said that since he had committed the sin of killing a cow, only Lord Shiva could help him atone.

An elderly sage: Then another rishi said to Gautam Rishi that if he had to atone for the killing of a cow, or Brahma Hatya, he would have to bring the Ganga here. The only God who could save him from this curse was Shiva. So he began the worship of Shiva. For thirty-six years, in stages of twelve years each, he worshipped Shiva, and suddenly He appeared before him and told him he would get whatever he desired.

Devotee 14: He said that he wanted the Ganga, which is tied in Shiva's hair, to come down to earth so he could bathe his sin away.

Devotee 15: Lord Shiva released the Ganga from His hair and from the mountains sprang the river, which in this area is known as the Godavari.

Juhi Chawla: The Godavari is also known as the Ganges of the South. Starting from the Kushavarth and finally ending in Bengal, the Godavari is one of the longest rivers in India. In our country, rivers have always been regarded as mothers.

Devotee 16: Godavari means the water (vari) that can nullify the sin of killing a cow. Here Godavari is famous as Gautami.

Devotee 17 (very old man): In Prayag and Haridwar, what Bhagirath Raja had brought down is known as Bhagirathi. This is the elder sister of Bhagirathi. That is why Kabir the poet has said. Godavari is the biggest Ganges.

Devotee 18: We honour and revere the Ganges a great deal.

Devotee 19: There are many people who come here, not only from our own country but from overseas as well. They bathe in the Godavari and say their prayers with piety.

Juhi Chawla: Kushavard Talav is the point from which Ma Godavari starts her journey. The Kumbh Mela, which is held every twelve years, starts from here. The Kumbha Mela started here at Kushavard Talav. Once, during a conflict between the gods and demons, when the ocean was being churned, the urn of nectar came to the fore. The gods chased the demons away but while leaving, droplets from the nectar fell in four places—Nashik, Allahabad, Ujjain and Haridwar. So every three years, the Kumbh takes place in each of these places.

A holy man: Gautam Rishi had bathed in the Godavari to atone for the sin of killing a cow. Similarly, all other saints come to bathe in the Godavari.

Juhi Chawla: The ambience of Trimbakeswar is soothing, appealing and beautiful. The Brahmagiri mountains are to the west, where the Godavari sprang to life. It is assumed to be the first peak of the Sahyadri range. Ascending, one can reach the Gangadwar, or the Doorway of the Ganges, which is the point from which the Godavari sprang to life. Here, the image of Goddess Ganga is established.

Devotee 20: The Ganga emerges from the Brahmagiri mountains. From there, in a hidden manner (unseen to people), it flows to Gangadwar. When it emerges from Gangadwar, it comes to Kushavard. By the power of Gautam

Rishi's incantation, he used a kush (grass) to bind a small part of the Godavari on four sides. Hence the name Kushvartha.

A priest: When someone bathes in Kushavard and goes to pay obeisance to the deity, it is assumed that his path will lead to moksha, or the ultimate bliss.

Juhi Chawla: The Trimbakeswar Temple is also regarded as the best place to offer prayers for the peace and ultimate release of our forefathers.

Devotee 21: After praying here, three children were born in our household.

A group of locals: For Hindus, this is regarded as the best place for performing obsequies, auspicious programmes, or just meditation and charity.

Devotee 22: My in-law passed away; it was an untimely death. Of the twelve Jyotirlingas, this is the best place to give his soul peace.

Devotee 23: We have come to worship Maharaj Bali, who resides in Patal Lok, or the Netherlands, because the sins of our ancestors which we are suffering now will come to an end.

Devotee 24: The Kaal sarp dosh is an astronomical calculation (dasha) which many people have in their birth charts (kundalis); this is believed to be malefic. If people worship here, it is believed that all impediments will vanish and there will be no problems in future. That is why I worship here.

Juhi Chawla: Millions of true believers have received the blessings of the Almighty here; this has enriched their lives and made them successful. That is also the reason why people continue to come here. Monday is regarded as especially auspicious, because it is regarded as the day dedicated to Lord Shiva. Should you happen to be in an auspicious place such as Trimbakeswar on a Monday, you should rejoice, as this is no less than any great festivity.

Every Monday, the palanquin of Trimbakeswar Maharaj carrying the five-faced gold façade of His image is taken around the village. This seems almost like the royal coronation of Lord Trimbakeswar. On festive or special occasions, the gold and diamond-studded crown of Lord Trimbakeswar is displayed for all devotees present. Devotees throng to this place to catch a glimpse of this.

Trimbakeswar is an auspicious place, where not only are all misconceptions of the mind cleared but prayers, too, derive a special force. When with such devotion and faith, a devotee expresses his heartfelt desire or pain or agony to Bholenath, He is bound to listen.

A little girl, with a child in her arms: In my opinion, if any person with all devotion and sincerity calls upon the Almighty, their prayers are bound to come true.

Man with wife and child: True religion is life. If you are true and good by religion, there will be no problems and your objectives will come true. If you just remain sitting and pray to Shiva to fulfil your wishes, it will not happen—you will have to work for it.

7

SAPTASHRUNGI TEMPLE

Considered to be as sacred as the Shakti peeths located across the Indian subcontinent, the Saptushrungi Devi Temple near Nashik is a sight to behold. Nestled among seven mountain peaks, the almost-ten-foot-high idol of Mata blesses the thousands of devotees who visit Her. Coated with sindoor and decorated with ornaments, one cannot miss Saptashrungi Mata's striking bright eyes that seem to dive deep into one's soul and light it up with faith from within.

Juhi Chawla: When there was nothing, He was omnipresent. When there will be utter emptiness, He will still be there. For aeons, people have an ingrained belief that there is a mystical power that has tied together so many millions of people. Sometimes with hands raised in faith and sometimes with hands folded in obeisance; sometimes carrying thalis of holy offerings, and at others bearing the holy books in faith—through these, all of us are engaged in a continual search for Him.

I, Juhi Chawla, will take you on such a sojourn, which is a unification of all such feelings, which traverses thousands of miles and draws people to the places where we may find Him. The experience of that faith, this journey, is of the conviction that we will.

Both the devotee and God remain incomplete without each other; it is all about belief and faith—the conviction that someone is there who controls everything. One just has to raise one's hands in supplication and gaze downwards, and all will be fulfilled.

Devotee 1: Taking Mother's name if we move forward, there will be no problems at all. Everything will be good.

Devotee 2: All our hopes and desires are fulfilled after coming here.

Devotee 3 (woman with an infant in her lap): My sister had pleaded for a child and her wish was granted. This is the child that we have brought here.

Devotee 4: A mother is a mother. She is a Goddess. There is a lot of joy and peace and happiness to be found here.

Juhi Chawla: At about 67 km from the Nashik district in Maharashtra, on a peak of the Sahyadri range, is located Saptashrungi Garh. This is the embodiment of belief and strength. The Saptashrungi Temple is a very potent pilgrim centre, with towering mountain peaks around. The steps of obeisance lead upwards, and to come face to face with that strength, climbing even 526 steps does not seem difficult.

Female ascetic: Is it possible for us to measure the power of the rays of the sun? Similarly, there is no measure of one's devotion. Whether a storm or a typhoon, there is always a crowd of devotees here.

Devotee 5: We look at her as the Mother, and as a mother She has strength. We should not come to ask for something but just to meet Her.

Juhi Chawla: On meeting Her and gazing up at Her, the head automatically bows in devotion, love and respect. It is like just to capture one glimpse of Her, our eyes close by themselves. This is the eternal power, Saptshrungi Mata.

Devotee 6: Ever since we can remember, we have been coming to see the Mother.

Devotee 7: I am from Nashik and have been coming here for the past ten or twelve years.

Devotee 8: I am from Surat.

Devotee 9 (elderly lady): We have been coming here for six generations—from the time of my great grandparents.

Devotee 10 (girl with a baby): I have been here for fifteen to twenty times, since my childhood. I have lost count, really.

Devotee 11: Many of our wishes have been fulfilled because we have come here so many times.

Mendicant: If we fall at Her feet, our wishes will come true.

Devotee 12 (old lady): We come to Her in reverence. If She calls, we come.

Female ascetic: Whatever anyone has wanted, the Mother has given them. That is why there is so much reverence for Her.

Devotee 13: We as women derive strength from Mother Saptashrungi.

Juhi Chawla: This Goddess with eighteen arms is believed to be another incarnation of Goddess Durga. That is why it is believed that with eighteen arms wide open, the Goddess showers love and blessings on all.

Devotee 14: My son, seventeen years old, is here only because of the blessings of the Goddess. It is from his earnings that we have come to collect the blessed food.

Devotee 15: I asked for blessings for my daughter's marriage and that was fulfilled.

Devotee 16: We wanted to build a house and we could get it done; there was another major task which also got completed.

Devotees 17: Whenever we come here, we bow down before the Goddess and our wishes come true.

Juhi Chawla: We ask for blessings, so that we get this beautiful world again and again. We get the warmth of Your love and the cradle of Your arms, O Mother. Different people, different prayers and appeals...

Sudarshan Anandrao Dahatonde (temple manager): The temple is situated in the Western Ghats, in Maharashtra. In the Ramayana, this is known as the Dandakaraya. When Lord Rama had to remain in hiding in the forest, he stopped here.

Juhi Chawla: Saptashrungi Devi is also known as the another form of Mahakali, Mahalakshmi and Mahasaraswati. She is regarded as the triumvirate of all that is good and pious in these three goddesses.

Dahatonde: Mahakali is the epitome of Parvati, Mahasaraswati is the wife of Brahma and Mahaklashmi is the wife of Vishnu. These three are seen in the form of the Mother.

Juhi Chawla: Devotees also regard this temple as Adhashaktipeeth. This means that it is worshipped with as much devotion and dedication as a Shakti peeth. Of course, it must be admitted that there is no allusion to be found about this, nor any reference. Due to its geographical location, Mata Shrungidevi is known by various names.

Dahatonde: This temple is known as Vani ki Mata. This is because at that time the path was a hilly one.

Old man: When I first started coming, there was no road here. One had to somehow clamber along. People used to stumble and fall.

Dahatonde: Then over a period of time, it came to be called Nandurigarh. At first, one would have to walk all the way from below. Now cars come up to this point. This happened about fifteen years ago, when the hilly road was developed into a proper one and all kinds of vehicles could get to the top, and then people began addressing it as the Saptashrungi Mata Temple. The naming happened in three phases. First, it was the Vani ki Devi (Goddess of Vani), then Nanduri ki Devi and now it's Saptashrungi Devi.

Juhi Chawla: There is always some festival or celebration on in this temple. But Navaratri has a very special place here.

There are six Navaratris in a year. In recent times, the number of devotees here have been raging between 50 lakhs and 60 lakhs.

Devotee 18 (elderly lady): We walk all the way from our village during Navaratri to catch a glimpse of the Goddess.

Devotee 19: The strength that is there in a goddess is not there in a god.

Devotee 20: We believe that a goddess stands for women's empowerment.

Devotee 21: If one looks at reality, the truth is just one— each of us has our own beliefs; we believe in the Goddess.

Juhi Chawla: Devotees might come from different corners of the World, but when they look upon the face of the Goddess, their devotion and piety make them all one. Ma Saptashrungi's ten-foot-tall image brings to the fore her heroic form and her intrinsic form of the Mother. Behind the Mother's valorous form is an extremely romantic tale from the scriptures—that of the demon Mahishasura and his killing. The devotees who plead for strength also narrate the mythological encounter of Mahishasur with Mata Saptshrungi.

Devotee 22: Mahishasura was a kind of demon. The Mother killed him. His head was like a buffalo's and his body was very broad.

Devotee 23: He was causing pain and discomfort to the entire universe—on Earth, in the underworld and even in heaven.

Devotee 24 (elderly man): There was a massive hole in the mountainside. He just kicked it open and ran away through it.

Priest: In the Kuru era, there was a fierce battle between the gods and the demons. Indra represented the gods and Mahishasura the demons. Mahishasura was so strong that he overcame Lord Indra and threw the gods out of heaven.

Female ascetic: No one could defeat him because of a boon he had been given by Brahma. But there was the clause that only a goddess could kill him.

Priest: So Brahma, Vishnu and Shiva combined their powers to create a Goddess. Mahishasura was killed here, in front of the temple of the Goddess.

Devotee 25 (old lady): After defeating the demons, the Goddess took her seat here.

Old ascetic lady: Her meditation was fierce.

Devotee 26: You can ask whatever you want from the Goddess.

Devotee 27 (young man): She is always the first to be worshipped.

Old ascetic lady: The Mother was happy and granted whatever was asked for. When we climb the stairs, it is Mahishasura who is worshipped first. It is because the Mother had killed Mahishasura that she is known as Mahishasurmardini.

Priest: If we look at South India, there are so many temples that are dedicated to Mahishasurmardini. But there is no temple in South India where Mahishasura is found. But in the Saptashrungi Temple, first it is the demon who attracts attention.

Juhi Chawla: There is another aspect to showcasing the grandeur of Saptashrungi Mata, which is her Shringar, or bathing and dressing ritual.

At 5.30 in the morning, after the temple doors are opened, the Kakad Aarti of the Mother is done. (Incantations chanted). This ten-foot image of Shrungimata, according to rituals, undergoes the Panchamrit bath. She is anointed with honey, sugar, milk, curd and clarified butter, and then with vermilion, and dressed in new clothes and jewellery. Her visage, with layers of vermilion, seems to bring to light the fiery form of the Goddess. Her glistening eyes are the very picture of love and affection.

The sun rises and the birds start chirping; the reverberation of worship and devotees overflow with love and respect. It is the belief of devotees that even before looking at the Mother, if they take a plunge in the waters of this holy reservoir, then not only the soiled body, but all that is unclean in the soul will turn pristine.

Sage: These waters are a blessing from Lord Shiva.

Sage 2: Devotees first come here to take a dip.

Man in saffron: Uncountable people take a dip here in this holy pond...

Old man: People come here from so many places, and it is vital to be clean and chaste before approaching the Goddess, so they wash their hands and feet in clean water; the mind remains as clean as the body. The importance of bathing in this pond is that the water not only cleanses the outer you but also the inner you, and thus you are ready to worship the Almighty.

Devotee 28: Whatever illness one might have is omitted from the body.

Holy man in saffron: If one bathes in the holy waters in the proximity of the Mother, any imminent danger is bypassed, and the soul is satisfied—which is why all come to bathe here.

Juhi Chawla: There is another meaning to immersing oneself in the holy waters—the attainment of supreme knowledge. It is in this manner that innumerable people have immersed themselves in devotion for the Mother and attained immeasurable knowledge. Of them one was Rishi Markendeya.

Priest: Rishi Markendeya is one of the most revered rishis or saints in history. It is believed that Markendeya was the son of a sage; he had been born because of a boon granted to the sage and his wife. However, his life had been granted only for fourteen years. So his parents sat in meditation to Lord Shiva once again and prayed with full faith and devotion. After a while, Shiva and Parvati appeared before them together and granted him a lifespan of 14 'kalp' (1 kalp = 1,000 years). So he was to live 14,000 years. This means a period even before that of the Ramayana and the Mahabharata.

Juhi Chawla: Rishi Markendeya, who was a true devotee of the Mother, composed the highly revered holy text, Durgasaptasati. This is part of the Markendeya Purana. This Durgasaptasati is regarded as highly important in the worship of the Mother, where she is described as Mahishasurmardini and the Mother of all Creation.

Manager of the temple trust: When Mahalakshmi took the form of Bhagwati (Saptashrungi) and killed Mahishasur, Markandey Rishi recited hymns in praise of Her, which calmed Her down. The mountain that you see in front is where Markandey Rishi prayed to the Goddess. When the incantation was over, the Mother leaned in to listen better and also in a relaxed fashion. This is the manner in which the Mother took form there.

Juhi Chawla: Whereas the enraged form of the Goddess is known as Mahishasurmardini, the Mother's serene and calm form is established in Vani and has come to be known as the Jagdamba Mata Mandir. 'Jagadamba' means the Mother of the Universe.

Admin priest: In Vani too, there is a temple dedicated to this form of the Goddess.

Juhi Chawla: The language in understanding one's faith might be different—words can be dissimilar, but feelings are one and the same. There is one bond.

Devotee 29 (woman carrying infant): I came here with utter devotion and there was no problem at all.

Devotee 30 (elderly lady): When there is a great deal of pain, it is essential that we fall at the feet of the Goddess. If there is pain, just take Her name and start walking.

Devotee 31 (sick lady): I am a diabetes patient, but even then I have no problems at all.

Devotee 32: There is trust, devotion and faith.

Devotee 33: The devotees who come here do so because of their faith. When someone sees the result of their faith and devotion, naturally they approach that strength.

Juhi Chawla: For some devotees, Saptashrungi Mata is the virtual epitome of life. For the locals here, She is also responsible for their livelihood. The better part of the people here earn money by selling vermilion, rudraksha and whatever else is needed in the worship of the Goddess.

Devotee 34: I had prayed to the Goddess for luck to my brother. My brother got a job in the BSF, and I am also prospering too.

Devotee 35: The Mother always ensures that we earn enough to keep ourselves fed.

Devotee 36: She ensures that we get by in our professions.

Devotee 37: If we have to know the ways of the world, then there must be an element of suspicion; however, if we want God, then belief is essential.

Juhi Chawla: It is as though the Mother says, 'I am with you, I am not far away, I am close by; I am not far away, I am near you. Close your eyes and focus on me—I am nothing but your own belief.'

8

RUMTEK DHARMA CHAKRA CENTRE

There's something about the hills that makes your heart yearn for a spiritual oneness with the Supreme. Perched on top of a gorgeous hill, around 24 km from the city of Gangtok in Sikkim is one such abode that fills your mind with the infinite gift of peace—the Rumtek Monastery. Belonging to the Kagyu sect of Buddhists, whose origins date back to twelfth-century Tibet, the Rumtek Monastery is known as the Dharma Chakra Centre. It consists of a beautiful shrine and the Nalanda Institute, for the monks who work selflessly towards learning and spreading the philosophy of Buddha across the world. An architectural design that can truly be termed one of the finest of its time, the Rumtek Dharma Chakra Centre has preserved stupas, murals and statues that make the monastery unique. Set amid majestic hills and breathtaking waterfalls, the Rumtek Monastery is a place where your soul attains peace in the truest sense.

Juhi Chawla: When there was nothing, He was omnipresent. When there will be utter emptiness, He will still be there. For aeons, people have an ingrained belief that there is a mystical power that has tied together so many millions of people. Sometimes with hands raised in faith and sometimes with hands folded in obeisance; sometimes carrying thalis of holy offerings, and at others bearing the holy books in faith—through these, all of us are engaged in a continual search for Him.

I, Juhi Chawla, will take you on such a sojourn, which is a unification of all such feelings, which traverses thousands of miles and draws people to the places where we may find Him. The experience of that faith, this journey, is of the conviction that we will.

Sikkim is a verdant, beautiful and refreshing state. There are innumerable treasures of nature hidden all over. The mountains seem to be singing a song of love and in the distance one can see beautiful tea gardens and hear the magical trickling of water. Someone seems to have woven a blanket of magic all around, which ties it all together.

Sikkim is home to some of the most beautiful monasteries in the world, one of which is situated 23 km from the capital, Gangtok. The Rumtek Monastery also known as the Rumtek Dharam Chakra Centre.

Devotee 1: When I first came here I was in Class V, and now I am studying in college. At that time, hardly anyone was here, but nowadays there are crowds of people coming here.

Devotee 2: This is a world-famous place and one feels a lot of peace after coming here.

Devotee 3: There is a lot of climbing that one has to do to get to the monastery. And I have understood why to some extent, the ego has to be left behind when coming here. After climbing so much, the peace and tranquillity are really worth seeing.

Devotee 4: The sound of the humming and chanting that can be heard from inside the monsastery brings peace to the mind.

Devotee 5 (a couple): There is a calm here that brings peace to the mind; it's a really good feeling.

Devotee 6: There are many new things to see, things I have never seen before. Overall the experience has been very good. This was the first time I had come and now I will think about coming here again and again.

Devotee 7: The literal meaning of Rumtek is 'valley top'. In the local dialect, 'rum' means God and 'tek' means place.

Juhi Chawla: This is the spot where the protective shadow of the Guru assumes the form of the shadow of the Almighty and showers blessings on all.

The words of the Guru, or the head of the monastery and the supreme teacher, have the power to bring us closer to the Almighty.

Devotee 8: When the holy songs are sung, the sound penetrates the inner being and we are transported from this world to another. That greatly appeals to me.

Devotee 9: There is a feeling of calm that settles on you as you sit in meditation with your eyes closed.

Devotee 10 (young man): It felt very good to be here and there was a sense of fulfilment. When you spend some time here, you find the solution to confusions and mysteries in life. You find peace of mind here.

Monk: If you are feeling sad or unhappy, then even an ordinary song will make you calm, happy and relaxed. If it is a mantra or a chanting that you find meaningful and which comes from devotion, there will be positive energy.

Juhi Chawla: The Rumtek Monastery symbolizes unending faith in Buddhist supreme teachings. This Buddhist monastery is one of the most ancient cultural centres too.

Monk: This monastery was constructed in 1960, and thereafter it was named the Dharma Chakra Centre. This monastery belongs to the Kagyu sect. The head is always Karmapa. 'Karma' here means duty. And duty is to spread religion.

Juhi Chawla: Karmapa is an incarnation of the Buddha. In all of his movements, there is a reflection of the Buddha. In the Tibetan tradition, there have been many such teachers who have had complete control over their actions in the past birth. Some such can be found even today, who had intimation of their births even before they were born.

Lama: I left home when I was four years old, and have been here in Sikkim since. I was a master in my previous life in Tibet in Joki Tasurphu Monastery. In this birth when I was two years old and living with my parents, the seventeenth Karmapa said that the lama had been reborn. He mentioned my name, that of my parents and the place where I was staying. He said that monks should go and look for me. So they came, they met my parents and realized that everything the monk had said was correct—so they brought me here.

Juhi Chawla: There are so many children who leave their homes and families behind, and stay under strict discipline at the Nalanda Institute in the Dharma Chakra Centre, undergoing training to grow up to be a lama or a Buddhist monk. Students there can avail of the opportunity of being taught by Tibetan gurus about Sutra, Tantra and Dhyana. After taking lessons, they can show others the right path to tread on.

Devotee 11: The Rumtek Monastery is actually a replica of a monastery in Tibet. It's a fine example of Tibetan architecture.

A frequent visitor: The architecture is fantastic, so much so that one can keep looking at it. It's colourful and beautiful, and there are a few things that you can relate to Hinduism and other cultures too.

Juhi Chawla: Each gompa, or Tibetan monastery, has a unique and different attraction. But one feature is the same in all—the picture of four gods in four directions at the main door. They are Virudhaka, Virupaksha, Vaishravan and Dhritrashtra.

When Guru Padmasambhava had finished preaching Buddhism, he gave responsibility to the four gods to protect Buddhism in their respective directions. They protect Buddhism and there is always a star above them—the Goddess of Wisdom. In the monastery you can also see a painting of Ganpatiji.

If on reaching the house of God, we are unable to communicate with Him, and He is unable to listen, how can faith grow? At the Rumtek Monastery, one can reach God through the wishing pole.

Monk: We call this pole 'doring' in Tibetan. 'Do' means stone and 'ring' means tall.

Devotee 12 (young girl): Get a chance to throw coins on the wishing pole; if the coin hits the pole within the given number of chances, then consider your wish fulfilled.

Devotee 13 (another young girl): Here, I have prayed that I fare well in my exams; and also that whatever is going on in my family gets sorted.

Devotee 14: A co-traveller prayed that a child who had lost her mother soon after birth is able to live her childhood with another mother. The coin fell in place, and I realized that the Buddha will make this dream come true.

Juhi Chawla: It is generally believed that from the outer ring, if the coin falls right inside, it has fallen into the lap of the Buddha. Of course, this is only a belief.

Monk: Even I do not know how it started, but the people who came here started throwing coins. Perhaps someone who had thrown a coin had their wish fulfilled. It might seem a bit strange to look at, but the motivation is pure. That is what matters.

Juhi Chawla: No matter what the path is or what the religion is, the desire of everyone is the same—peace of mind.

Devotee 15: Lord Buddha is a saint. Everyone who believes in peace, in Dharma, and wants peace and tranquillity can come here.

Devotee 16: Buddhism is mysticism and religion both. Even if we have everything, we are not happy. No matter what we have, we keep running around looking for more in this physical world. But coming here, we get peace. Look at the life you are leading—you have everything but you are not happy. Like Gautam Buddha, leave everything and become unattached—there is a lot of peace in that.

Juhi Chawla: In Buddhism, prayers mainly mean finding the Buddha within us. But one has to search for the inner Buddha and the difficulty in doing so is that one is searching someone who is already within, hence the seeker is a Buddha too. The motivation is the same, as is the goal. If the palms are brought together, it is not to ask for something, but to search for the inner Buddha within oneself.

Monk: Performing a puja means doing something good, something positive. The results that we get from this, the merits that we garner, we distribute among others.

Juhi Chawla: Mandalas spread positivity. Mandalas are the palace of the deities. Just like a mandala, Tibetan Vajrayana (a kind of Buddhism predominant in the Himalayan nations of Tibet, Nepal, Bhutan and Mongolia, called so because of the ritual use of Vajra, a symbol of an imperishable diamond) is taken to be an extremely fulfilling concept.

Monk: When we try to do something good or positive, there are a lot of obstacles. To prevent these obstacles from coming in our way, we perform offerings. If there is a beginning, there is also an end. To always keep this in mind, at the end, the mandala is wiped out. Whatever religious structures are made are broken in the end. But only the external objects are wiped away, not the foundation of spirituality. All prayers are for peace, and we pray for others—let all that is good happen to others and let there be good for the world. Religious work is done for the benefit of others. There is great compassion for others.

The Buddha said that if a conscious being is full of natural love and compassion, his mind can be called pure. The firmament is always present, so are the sun, stars and moon; but sometimes clouds can shroud them and we cannot see them—but that does not mean they are not there. The path that the Buddha showed us is also right there for us to follow. The Buddha said, 'I chose this path and got there. If all of you do the same, you will also get there.'

Juhi Chawla: The core of all Buddhist prayers is 'Om Mani Padme Hum'. It is believed that on pronouncing this incantation, Karuna ka Dev (God of Compassion), Avalokesteswar, is bound to cast His glance of love and empathy at you. It is a simple incantation, but it includes the core of all prayers within it.

Foreign devotee: My doctor had told me that I had a very bad disease. But then I visited the monastery. When my doctor operated on me, he was kind of disappointed, because he didn't find anything. I think it was the mantra at the monestery that worked.

Monk: The mantra is very powerful, because these are not ordinary words and it is not an ordinary message. It is a message directly from the Buddha. It is the sound of the Avalokesteswar. So we chant the mantra, which is extremely powerful. It is because of this that anger vanishes, and calm and peace reigns. When compassion becomes greater, then peace and everything that is good reigns...

Juhi Chawla: When we reach such a powerful place as the Rumtek Monastery, we are compelled to take a look at our inner selves. Gautam Buddha himself had said that the ultimate truth hidden in Him helped Him distinguish between right and wrong. This truth takes us along the path of life, which is truthful and joyous.

Devotee 17: The main advantage of meditation is that our minds remain in control.

Devotee 18: Meditation helps us focus our mind on one point, and then peace and happiness is ours.

Devotee 19: We learn to recognize ourselves, focus on our inner thoughts, and concentrate on our breathing; our healing powers and good thoughts increase; no matter how chaotic the atmosphere is, we still manage to feel good and, because of us, the people around us also feel the positive energy.

Monk: Once you understand the nature of your own mind, your mind will be clear and you will become the Buddha.

Devotee 20 (young man): I believe Buddhism, Hinduism, Jainism and Islam are all the same. I am taking back peace of mind, good memories and self-fulfilment from here.

Devotee 21: Money, no matter how much you have, will not make you happy. Actual happiness is within yourself.

Devotee 22: We should be truthful to ourselves, and then everything becomes easy, simple and peaceful.

Juhi Chawla: All that you see and hear in the gompa resonates with the Buddha... Devotion and prayers are what unite us with the Buddha. All differences can be destroyed to make us the Buddha.

9

UDUPI

About 60 km from the city of Mangaluru is the peaceful hamlet Udupi. Located here is a quaint math of Lord Sri Krishna, a holy place for thousands of devotees who throng here to shower love on their favourite lord. The idol of Lord Krishna sits here in child-like innocence. Swathed in fragrant garlands and brilliant gold-lined garments, the beatific idol casts a spell of happiness the moment you set eyes on it. Devotees who visit the Sri Krishna Math strongly believe that faith and sacredness get redefined within the confines of this ashram.

Juhi Chawla: When there was nothing, He was omnipresent. When there will be utter emptiness, He will still be there. For aeons, people have an ingrained belief that there is a mystical power that has tied together so many millions of people. Sometimes with hands raised in faith and sometimes with hands folded in obeisance; sometimes carrying thalis of holy offerings, and at others bearing the holy books in faith—through these, all of us are engaged in a continual search for Him.

I, Juhi Chawla, will take you on such a sojourn, which is a unification of all such feelings, which traverses thousands of miles and draws people to the places where we may find Him. The experience of that faith, this journey, is of the conviction that we will.

Devotee 1: If we come here there is peace, otherwise there is a feeling of restlessness.

Devotee 2 (young girl sitting with two children): The place of God is very pious; there is a feeling of the strength of God, and then comes a feeling of relaxation. It's not like sitting at home and watching television!

Devotee 3 (young man): There is a positive ambience here.

Devotee 4 (young couple): This is a place where you are bound to find peace, regardless of how difficult your life is.

Juhi Chawla: In the Shrimad Bhagavad Gita, Sri Krishna says that it is only through devotion that one can know God.

Devotee 5: I can feel Sri Krishna every single day. This bond between God and his devotees seems to increase every day.

Juhi Chawla: Sri Krishna is worshipped as the eighth incarnation of Lord Vishnu. That is why Udupi is also known as Vaikunth, the pious locale of Lord Vishnu Himself. Devotees of all ages throng this place.

Devotee 6: I have come from Mumbai.

Two foreigners: We have come from San Diego, in California, the United States.

Young man with son: I have been coming here since I was his age, about four.

Lady holding a child in her arms: We feel the presence of God here and that is why people come here from great distances.

Middle-aged lady: Whatever problems there are at home are resolved when we come here. I believe in Lord Krishna.

Elderly man: There is no place that lacks the presence of the Almighty.

Juhi Chawla: At a distance of about 60 km from Mangaluru is located a divine pilgrim centre, Udupi. It is also known as the Temple City. Of all the temples located here, the most famous is the Sri Krishna Math.

Sri Krishna Math is such a holy place that devotion flows through it like a lilting stream. All those who come for a glimpse of their beloved Krishna is filled with love and piety. This holy ground is also the birthplace of the renowned thinker Sri Madhva Acharya. Sri Krishna Math was established by him. In the Tulu language, 'Udupi' is also pronounced 'Udapa'. Numerous meanings can be unearthed from this.

Holy man in saffron: 'Udupa' means a constellation and the ruler of the constellation is the Moon. That is why it is known as Udupi. Madhva Acharya was aware that the Moon had been worshipped at this spot, and therefore the temple was established here—and even now we can see Lord Krishna here.

Elderly man in saffron: 'Udupa' means a small child. Here, the image of Lord Krishna is also that of a child. The idol of Krishna is also Udupa.

Juhi Chawla: In the ancient Udupi temple, Lord Krishna is seen in His serene, infant form. His beautiful form decorated in jewels steals the heart. The reason for His presence here in infant form has a very interesting story behind it. Narrations like this make our love for Him grow even deeper. According to a tale from the Puranas, Mother Devaki once requested Lord Krishna to allow her to have a glimpse of the childhood that He had spent in Gokul. Hearing His mother, Sri Krishna again took the form of a child and showed her all the antics of His childhood.

Sri K. Ramachandra Bhatt (assistant dewan at the Sri Krishna Math): Devaki stated that she had not seen His childhood because He had been with Yashoda Ma. So to bring this forth, He took the form of a child. He grabbed the rope that Devaki Ma was using to make butter after milking the cows and ran away. Devaki chased after him, while Rukmini Devi observed all this from behind a door.

Juhi Chawla: Seeing this child-like form, there were no limits to the joy Rukmini felt. She felt hypnotized.

Bhatt: One day she said that she wanted an image of Child Krishna that Rukmini could worship. He made such an image and gave it to Rukmini, who began worshipping it.

Juhi Chawla: It is believed that when Sri Krishna finally departed, He left a similar image in Dwarka. Then this image reached Udupi on the vessel of a businessman.

H.R. Srinath (seva officer of the Sri Krishna Math): A

business vessel from North India, probably from Dwarka, was caught in a massive storm. The people on board began pleading for their lives and in order to restore the balance, began gathering clumps of mud on the vessel.

The famous thinker Madhva Acharya rescued the drowning ship. The ship owner offered him any or all the precious items on the ship. But Madhva Acharya took only the idol of Sri Krishna in child form.

Young ascetic in saffron: Madhva Acharya through his divine insight had come to know that it was the image of Sri Krishna that Rukmini Devi had seen. He brought it and after keeping it immersed in the Madhav Sarovar for forty-eight days, had it established in the temple.

Juhi Chawla: Here at the Sri Krishna Math, the procedure of catching a glimpse of the image of Sri Krishna in the womb of the temple is unique. This is done through a very small window, divided into nine square parts. It is known as the Nab Griha Kindi.

Srinath: Remember how small or minute you are. Unless you focus keenly, you will not be able to see Him. This is known as Nava Dwar, or the nine doors. Looking for God in this manner perhaps cannot be found in any other temple of India.

Juhi Chawla: Even one day spent on these auspicious premises is sure to fill you with immeasurable joy and happiness. Every once in a while, the doors of the Nab Griha are thrown open. At that time, all devotees become overwhelmingly eager to catch a glimpse of their beloved Kanha, or Sri Krishna.

Devotee 7: By peering through the window and trying to

catch a glimpse of the Lord is indeed a great feeling.

Devotee 8: It is a beautiful sensation—it feels like the Lord Himself is standing in front of you. You feel like you are so close to God; there is no thought other than Him. It is a very beautiful idol.

Devotee 9: One feels like staying there. There is nothing I want but to stay in Udupi.

Juhi Chawla: In the Bhagavat Purana, Sri Krishna says that if anyone feeds cows and is friendly with them, they will unknowingly be bonding with Him.

Devotee 10: All devotees who come here themselves can perform 'go-daan', or offering of a cow and a calf to the Lord. This means that a cow and a calf are brought in front of the Lord, are decorated, worshipped and fed, and are then given as a gift to Him.

Juhi Chawla: Gopala is another name for Sri Krishna. It means the one who tends to cows and protects them. It is believed that as a young boy, Sri Krishna was so loving towards them that the cows would fuss more over him than over their own calves.

Devotee 11 (young girl): We feel a lot of happiness when we hear about Sri Krishna. He looks so nice, and whatever we pray for is almost always fulfilled.

Devotee 12: He is a great god; He is our God. There is nothing beyond Him.

Juhi Chawla: Another major attraction of the Sri Krishna Math is that directly in front of the mantapa is the ancient

Gopura Stambh (dome). Just below it is a window, known as the Kanak Das Kindi.

Kanak Das was a talented and popular saint, poet and musician of the sixteenth century. He was a scholar and a philosopher. But the most important factor was that he was a great devotee of Sri Krishna. That was such an era that people of the lower castes were forbidden to enter temples. Kanak Das remained immersed in the love and devotion to his God, in the hope that he would be permitted to enter the temple sometime or the other and be able to see his God for himself. However, this did not happen, and then one day there was a miracle.

Devotee 13: An earthquake resulted in the west wall cracking, and the image of Sri Krishna turned from facing the door to facing the cracked wall. Hence Kanak Das was able to get a glimpse of his beloved God.

Juhi Chawla: Later, in the cracks that had appeared on the wall, a window was constructed, which came to be known as the Kanak Das Kindi. This is proof of true devotion and, just like Kanak Das, innumerable devotees come here to feel close to their Lord.

Devotee 14: There is a lot of strength in Him. So, if we pray to God, it should be from the heart. If we truly pray to the Lord and call upon Him from the heart, we are sure to have peace of mind.

Devotee 15: I see Lord Krishna in my dreams often. If I am faced with any problem, He resolves all of them and shows me the right path to follow.

Juhi Chawla: Towards the rear of the math, there is a reservoir of water, known as the Madhav Sarovar. It is a different feeling altogether when, at the break of dawn, before going to pray to the Lord with a heart full of devotion, people take a dip in the Madhav Sarovar. Everything around seems to flower with the beauty of their piety and love. Devotees believe in the holy power of the Madhav Sarovar, that bathing here cleanses them of all sin.

Devotee 16: In the Madhav Sarovar, when you take a bath with promise and resolve in mind, you will have a promising rebirth and will achieve the Ultimate Brahma—his coming births will be blessed and he will attain Brahma Gyan (ultimate knowledge or enlightenment). The waters of the Madhav Sarovar are truly sanctified.

Devotee 17: If we bathe in the Madhav Sarovar, all our diseases will be washed off. So we have a bath in the Madhav Sarovar and also use it for worship.

Juhi Chawla: The fact is that if we bathe in the sarovar, it is as good as bathing in the Ganges. This is not mere talk but an undeniable truth that has come to us through generations.

Vasudeva Bhatt (public relations officer of the Sri Krishna Math): The Madhav Sarovar has been described by all the haridasas (holy men dedicated to Sri Krishna/Vishnu)—Madhvacharya, Kanak Das, Puran Das and Vadhiraja—and other great men. Haridasas especially described the power of the Padmasarovara (Madhav Sarovar). All the haridasas have said that once in twelve years the River Ganges will return.

Devotee 18: As the haridasas said that Ganga will be present in the Madhav Sarovar every twelve years, taking a dip in it is equivalent to taking a dip in the Ganga.

Juhi Chawla: The tradition of donation of food is followed here. Every morning and evening, food is served to devotees, which all accept as blessed food of the Lord.

Ascetic: Udupi is renowned for Anna Brahma (God of food).

Devotee 19: When the stomach is full, the manner of working changes. All that one desires is fulfilled. People talk of a sound body and a sound mind—a sound mind is got from a glimpse of God and a sound body is got from partaking of his blessed food.

Juhi Chawla: There is another renowned tradition here. Every Saturday, instead of food being served on banana leaves, it is served directly on the mat that has been laid out, which is savoured by devotees, who believe that whatever their heartfelt desires are will be fulfilled.

Devotee 20 (young girl): We eat from the floor and not from thalis.

Devotee 21: I had broken my hand, but even then I sat on the floor and partook of food. My broken hand miraculously healed.

Juhi Chawla: It is believed that the one who can offer to the Lord true devotion and belief is the greatest worshipper of all. Even then, the Lord being worshipped in accordance with all rituals and procedures plays a very important role. This ritualistic worship has been carried out for the past 800 years.

Sri Krishna is worshipped fourteen times a day in Udupi.

Incantations of the 108 names of Sri Krishna are chanted every day. Blessed food and ritualistic prayers are offered. After this, the decorated image of the infant Sri Krishna is placed in an ornate and bedecked palanquin and taken around for the devotees to look at.

This seems to be the time when all devotees lovingly carry the infant Krishna and take Him out and shower Him with love. This palanquin is pulled by the devotees themselves.

Immersed in the love of the Lord, the desire to see Him becomes intense. When this intensity becomes a longing for the Lord, when this longing becomes an acute inspiration to attain Krishna Consciousness, then it is to be understood that the journey of moving towards Sri Krishna has started.

Foreign devotee: During the course of the kirtans, or devotional songs, the chants 'Hare Krishna' are incomparable. This is something I have never experienced before.

Devotee 22: I pray that each and every devotee feels the touch of Sri Krishna and that Krishna Consciousness is always with him.

10

DAKSH MAHADEV TEMPLE

A place that literally means the Gateway to God, Haridwar is considered one of the holiest places for Hindus. Located on the banks of the Ganga, Haridwar has been the centre of the Hindu religion and mysticism for centuries. Legend has it that during the Samudra Manthan, Haridwar, along with Ujjain, Nashik and Allahabad, were the places where drops of amrit (elixir of immortality) accidentally spilt while being carried by Garuda. This is celebrated by holding the Kumbh Mela once in every twelve years here. The exact spot where the drops of amrit fell is known as Har ki Pauri (footsteps of the Lord) and it is a strong belief among the Hindus that taking a dip in these ghats can wash away one's sins and help one attain moksha (salvation). The luminous and reverberant Ganga aarti that takes place every evening on the ghats of Haridwar is a sight to behold. The most famous temple of Haridwar, which is also one of its identity markers, is the Daksheshwar Mahadev Temple.

Located around 5 km from Har ki Pauri, the temple is considered the source of all fifty-two Shakti peeths in the world. Mythological scriptures hint at the fact that King Daksh was one of the fourteen Prajapatis (creator deities), and also the father of Sati, who was married off to Lord Shiva in a lavish ceremony here. Known for his arrogance, King Daksh wasn't very fond of Lord Shiva, and hence Sati immolated herself in one of the kunds during a yajna. An angry Lord Shiva then manifested as a self-created linga and ordered the severing of Daksha's head, but later replaced it with the head of a male goat so that the yajna could proceed peacefully. Then Lord Shiva declared that every year, during the month of Saavan, the month that was dearest to the Lord, Kankhal would be His abode. Rich in history and laden with the divine powers of Lord Shiva, Daksheshwar Mahadev Temple will surely bind your soul to the supreme.

Juhi Chawla: When there was nothing, He was omnipresent. When there will be utter emptiness, He will still be there. For aeons, people have an ingrained belief that there is a mystical power that has tied together so many millions of people. Sometimes with hands raised in faith and sometimes with hands folded in obeisance; sometimes carrying thalis of holy offerings, and at others bearing the holy books in faith—through these, all of us are engaged in a continual search for Him.

I, Juhi Chawla, will take you on such a sojourn, which is a unification of all such feelings, which traverses thousands of miles and draws people to the places where we may find

Him. The experience of that faith, this journey, is of the conviction that we will.

I'm in search of myself, but who am I looking for? I have everything, then why this feeling of despair? Please stop me and bring me into your fold. I am a small speck and you are the entire firmament. Uttarakhand is known as Devbhoomi, or Land of the Gods, and the entrance to this hallowed land is Haridwar. It is the home of untrammelled faith. The devotee finds peace here and comes even closer to Bholenath (Shiva).

Devotee 1: This is the Siddhipith Bhoomi of Lord Shiva. If devotees come here with true faith, Lord Shiva will surely fulfil their wishes and desires.

Devotee 2: All my desires have been fulfilled after coming here. Whatever I have has been given by Him.

Devotee 3: I have been coming here with my parents ever since I was a child, and so this place holds great significance for me. Now my parents are no longer alive; but whenever I feel heavy-hearted, I come here—for me this is the best place to find peace.

Devotee 4 (young girl): The very name of the place— Haridwar, or 'Hari ka dwar' (the doorway to Shiva)—fills one with a sense of peace.

Devotee 5 (young man): Just look at God, find Him reflected in your heart and you will get everything.

Devotee 6 (middle-aged couple): Haridwar and Rishikesh are taken to be part of the four important pilgrim centres in India.

Juhi Chawla: The greatness of this pilgrim centre is hidden in the name itself. Haridwar is among the holiest places in India, and the entry point to Kedarnath, Badrinath, Gangotri and Yamunotri. This holy place has been visited by a lot of holy men, saints and sages.

Devotee 7: King Sagar's ancestors were cursed to ashes by Kapil Muni. Bhagirath then prayed to Ganga to come down to Earth. Lord Shiva then bound Her in His tresses to cut down Her ferocity and released just the requisite amount to reach the earth. This freed the ancestors' souls from Kapil Muni's curse. Har ki Pauri is the place where it all happened. For Hindus, when there is a death in the family, the ashes have to be brought here for immersion.

Devotee 8 (elderly man): I come here to pray for the peace of departed souls; and I find that peace here.

Devotee 9: When the soul travels to meet his maker, this is where he comes. So this is known as Haridwar.

Juhi Chawla: This place is a bridge to moksha. The Ganga river is one of belief, where devotees can traverse the bridge of life with loving care.

Devotee 10: The flowing water of the Ganga is regarded as holy. All flaws and negative elements are washed away in those who bathe in these waters.

Devotee 11: When we come to Haridwar and bathe in these holy waters, not only do we add to our good deeds, we also nullify the bad deeds we may have accumulated.

Devotee 12: It is like a thief, but one who steals our bad deeds. I do not even realize how my sins have vanished after I finish bathing. Hari ka dwar—that means it is like his lap.

Devotee 13: When we bathe in these waters, we experience a different kind of tranquillity.

Devotee 14: It is a different form of the Almighty and in His lap we feel blessed.

Devotee 15: It feels very good to come here for a dip in the Ganga.

Devotee 16: I felt a great deal of peace and I was able to bathe with a great deal of love; I even drank plenty of the holy water.

Juhi Chawla: This place is a unique mingling of history, religion and faith. The ancient roots of this place are just as powerful as its strength and ambience. This can be felt in every nook and corner.

Devotee 17 (elderly man): During the Sagar Manthan, Basukinath was wrapped firmly around a mountain peak and used to churn the ocean. As a result of this, fourteen jewels were found but also poison, which Shiva drank. Amrit was one of the results of the churning. When amrit came to the fore, there was a fight between the gods and the demons for its possession. This continued for twelve days—in human terms that is twelve years.

Devotee 18 (middle-aged man): The demons thought that if they got hold of the nectar, they would become eternally powerful and then no one would be able to destroy them. So the gods—Jayant, the son of Indra Dev, Dev Guru Brihaspati,

Surya Dev and Chandrama—sneakily managed to steal the nectar and run away with it. When they felt tired, they would put the pitcher down for a while and then again start running. When they would put their pitcher down, a few drops would spill over. In the course of their flight, they put the pitcher down in four places—Allahabad, Ujjain, Nashik and Haridwar. That is why the Kumbh Mela ('kumbh' means pitcher) takes place in these four places.

Juhi Chawla: You live in every single drop
You are my Lord
You turn poison into nectar
As long as you are with me.

Seeing the faithful crowds at the Har ki Pauri Ghat and the dips they take in the water, it seems as if Ma Ganga herself is carrying the message of trust and love to the Almighty.

Devotee 19: All our sins are washed away the moment we take a bath in these waters.

Devotee 20 (young girl): The aarti or ceremonial worship of Ma Ganga is so positive. There is something in it that makes the prayers spring from the heart.

Priest: There are special prayers chanted along the Ganga—at 5.30 in the morning.

Devotee 21: In this worship, 1,101 leaves are used. Devotees who happen to be in the temple at that time participate in the ceremonies. On the banks of the Ganga, the priest, with eleven Brahmins, makes arrangements for an appropriately honourable worship of the Goddess. And in the end comes the aarti.

Devotee 22: Performing the aarti increases our faith in Her and brings us blessings from Her.

Devotee 23 (young man): It is a blessing even to witness the blessings of Ma Ganga.

Devotee 24: Peace comes only through prayers and devotional songs; a man can never forget what gives his soul peace. Last evening, after participating in the aarti, I felt so much peace. That is why I come here—to fill the pitcher of faith and light the lamp of life. The Lord has taken away all my sins and listened to what my heart had to say.

Juhi Chawla: Haridwar is a place of staunch faith and there is an abundance of temples and holy relics close by. About 5 km from Har ki Pauri, the Daksh Mahadev Mandir of Kankhalcan be found.

Devotee 25: We have come from Delhi.

Devotee 26 (foreign tourist): I am from Istanbul, Turkey.

Devotee 27 (mother with a small child): I have been coming here since I was a child.

Devotee 28: I have been coming here for the past fourteen–fifteen years; it could even be twenty years!

Devotee 29: Whenever I have asked people which place we should visit, almost everybody has advised us to come here, and that is why we are here. And it feels really good.

Devotees 30 (elderly couple): We have come from afar and performed the puja here. Now both of us have been purified and enlightened.

Devotee 31 (young boy): I do not ask for anything, but to just pray that my life remains simple.

Juhi Chawla: Shiva is the solution to all problems. He is the donor of riches and joys. Under Lord Shiva's protection, it feels like all ties have been severed. The mind is set free and everything that we see appears to be Mount Kailash.

Devotee 32: I have asked for blessings for our son. It is our hope and desire that our son becomes a doctor and serves needy people.

Devotee 33: There is no need to ask Him for anything. All you have to do is ask Him to show you the way.

Devotee 34 (elderly man): My family faced a great crisis, and we had to face it all alone. There was not only shortage of money, but my health, too, suffered a great deal. He was the only one with me. Bholenath rescued me from that...

Juhi Chawla: People from all over the world come here to pay homage to the Lord and bow at the threshold of the Daksheshwar Mahadev Temple. In historical perspective and in the Puranas, the temple is a very important part of Haridwar.

Devotee 35: Daksh was the king of the Brahmand, or the universe. He is considered the child of Shiva.

Vivek Pokhriyal (sevak or servitor of the temple): Kankhal is important because it was the prime land of Daksh. Raja Daksh used to live here, and Ma Sati was also born here. Lord Shiva, along with thirty-three kinds of gods, goddesses, deities, demons and ghosts as his wedding procession, came here to marry Ma Sati. Thus the importance of this place.

Juhi Chawla: Raja Daksh was known to have been a vain king, who belittled Shivji in every way. But thanks to the greatness of Shivji, even the king became his greatest follower and devotee. This act of Shiva and the example of Daksh is dedicated to this Kankhal Daksheshwar Mahadev Temple.

Maharaj Daksh was against Shiva. He felt this way because he was the overlord of Brahmand and Shiva kept the company of all manner of ghosts and spirits, spent a large part of his time in cemeteries and partook of intoxicants. Daksh intensely disliked these traits.

Devotee 36: Daksh Prajapati made arrangements for a massive yajna, but did not invite Shiva. But Shiva's wife, and Daksha's daughter, Sati, stubbornly insisted on going. Shiva consented but refused to go himself. On reaching the yajna, Sati asked where the throne for her husband was. Raja Daksh replied there was none.

Vishweshwar Puri (manager of the temple): In the midst of all kings and luminaries present, this insult to her husband Shiva could not be tolerated by Sati and she set herself on fire. Her body turned to ashes. When Shivji got to know of this, He tore a strand of His hair and sent a demon to Daksh. This demon destroyed everything and severed Daksh's head from his body and threw it into the burning fire.

Shiva then picked Sati up in His arms and flew up into the firmament. Guru of the gods Brihaspati advised that Sati be removed from His arms. Vishnu said that His Sudarshan Chakra would act in just the manner He ordered. The Sudarshan Chakra then divided Sati's body into fifty-two parts. The fifty-two places where these parts fell became the Shakti peeths.

In the courtyard of this temple is situated the Sati Kund, the foundation stone (Aadhar Shila) of all Shakti peeths.

Juhi Chawla: It is believed that this is the very peeth where Sati self-immolated.

Devotee 37 (elderly man): After the incident, when Shiva returned to the place again, Sati's mother fell at His feet and begged Him to forgive her husband. Daksh's head had been replaced with that of a goat. Then it became clear to Daksh that there was no one greater than Shiva. Daksh asked Shiva for a boon—to allow his name to not get lost in time, and that he would pray to Shivji, his son-in-law.

Juhi Chawla: Shiva is not just a name, but a divine incantation that is the truth. All fear His rage, but behind it lies a divine child-like innocence that lights up the entire world. Shiva knows the power of forgiveness, just as Daksh realized. This is the assurance that every devotee counts on when coming here.

Devotee 38 (young girl): It is unlikely that any other deity will fulfil your desires as quickly as Shivji does.

Devotee 39: The first avatar of the divine is none other than Shiva, or Shankar.

Devotee 40: He is known as Bhole Bhandari because He fulfils all your needs.

Juhi Chawla: It is believed that even one flower offered with reverence is equal to an entire garden. Just as His divinity is simple, so are the means of worshipping Him.

Devotee 41: We made offerings of rice, milk and coins—whatever we could we offered in reverence.

Devotee 42: The dhatura flower is offered to Shankar Bhagwan (Lord Shiva) and the leaves of the bel flower are strung together.

Devotee 43 (young man): Shankar Bhagwan is very fond of consuming the dhatura (a type of fruit which can be poisonous) and intoxicants, which is heat-inducing. Further, it is also believed that if the heat becomes too overpowering, His third eye opens, and that could mean the destruction of the world. That is why He is also offered sandal, which has a cooling effect, and water is poured on Him twenty-four hours. He will then be kind and take pity on us all.

Devotee 44 (mother with daughters): He is our mother and father; so what can we offer Him? But if we make Him any offering we can, but with pure reverence, He accepts it with kindness and is satisfied.

Juhi Chawla: Offerings are symbols of love and reverence, and made to their beloved Bholenath with wholehearted devotion. During the aarti, with the sound of conch shells being blown and other musical instruments, it feels as though the air is redolent with vermilion and all things divine. Voices are raised in joy and reverence forms a carpet of faith. On that soft and silken layer, with the trident in His hand and swinging His pellet drum, with the Ganga captured in His locks, Shiva arrives to be with all His devotees.

11

MAHALAKSHMI TEMPLE

It is said that a mother is the Almighty, able to love infinitely. She can tend a broken heart and can rebuild life out of ruins; she is a place of hope. Millions from across the country come to Kolhapur for a glimpse of this energy, this hope in the form of an image mounted on a stone platform, carved in black. She is the Goddess Mahalakshmi of Kolhapur, considered to be the reason for the prosperity of this city, bringing crowds to the temple at all times of the day!

Juhi Chawla: When there was nothing, He was omnipresent. When there will be utter emptiness, He will still be there. For aeons, people have an ingrained belief that there is a mystical power that has tied together so many millions of people. Sometimes with hands raised in faith and sometimes with hands folded in obeisance; sometimes carrying thalis of holy offerings, and at others bearing the holy books in faith—through these, all of us are engaged in a continual search for Him.

I, Juhi Chawla, will take you on such a sojourn, which is a unification of all such feelings, which traverses thousands of miles and draws people to the places where we may find Him. The experience of that faith, this journey, is of the conviction that we will.

You are the mother; You are the one who takes care of us all. Life itself is a gift from You, the innocence of childhood; You brim over with love and nurturing.

Devotee 1: This temple is akin to my mother. Everybody discarded me, but this temple never did.

Devotee 2: Just as a mother cradles a child in her lap, She, too, does the same for us. It feels like we have come home to our mother. My mother is not alive (points towards the skies). She is my mother.

Devotee 3 (young man, weeping): I get so overwhelmed that I feel like weeping... I don't have words...

Devotee 4: It appeals a great deal to me and I feel like crying, because Ma was kind enough to call me and permit me to look upon Her.

Devotee 5 (middle-aged man): I do not feel like leaving this place—Ma has ensconced herself so firmly in my heart.

Devotee 6: There is nothing that I want from Ma, except that She allow me to come here. That is enough for me. I feel happy to see so many devotees around.

Devotee 7: If there is no faith, there is nothing. With belief even a stone can be God; but without it, it will always be a mere stone. Then there is no meaning at all. Faith is everything.

Juhi Chawla: At a distance of 400 km from Mumbai is situated Kolhapur. Also renowned as Karveer, this place is known for the Panchganga River and its antiquated buildings and ancient folklore.

Devotee 8 (young man): Panchganga rises in the south and flows towards the north. But the place where it turns once again to the south is known as Soth Kashi, or Karveer.

Devotee 9: The home of a million gods is in Karveer.

Devotee 10: Karveer is a place of hope and happiness during one's lifetime, and a place of peace and freedom after death, thanks to the blessings of Jagadamba.

Juhi Chawla: Karveer is a vibrant centre of Ma Adi Shakti. To that, the offering of Ma Mahalakshmi Temple is made.

Devotee 11: There is no better fortune than being able to get a glimpse of the Goddess. A motive of one's existence seems fulfilled if he is able to pay respects to the Goddess. It so happens that for us each day begins here.

Devotee 12 (young woman): When we bow before the Mother, there is a different kind of peace altogether.

Devotee 13 (elderly man): Coming here, one finds peace. People say that God is everywhere, but to me, She is only to be found in this temple. Till you actually go to the temple, you will not find peace. Remain at home and you will find quietude, but not peace.

Devotee 14: It feels like we have come very close to Ma. There are wondrous feelings and positive vibrations. When we go back to Mumbai, we are full of energy.

Devotee 15: There are no negative vibrations here. I have come here so my entire being can be recharged. Even as I am narrating this, I am getting goosebumps.

Devotee 16: I come here at 8.00 in the morning and gaze at Ma. Then I pay my respects to Her and begin my day.

Devotee 17: As long as I am alive, I will serve Ma.

Juhi Chawla: You are the very life of your devotees. I continue to breathe because of You and will never let go of Your aanchal (portion of sari draped over the shoulder). Hopes and desires flower here.

Devotee 18: I was extremely poor. And it's been a while that I've been coming here. Now all is well at home and my children go for work regularly. I like it a lot.

Devotee 19: I have undergone a brain tumour operation. It is my firm belief that Ma will shower great kindness on me.

Devotee 20: All devotees, especially those who are worried and concerned, have an inherent faith that their sorrows will be lessened. All wishes are fulfilled here. That is why people throng here.

Devotee 21 (middle-aged woman): Ever since I was very young, each Navaratri I have been coming here.

Devotee 22 (middle-aged man): Once a month does not suffice, so I come here twice a month.

Devotee 23: This place is surrounded by positive vibes, and they help us grow.

Devotee 24 (young girl): Even if we pray at home, vibrations will reach the temple. But the blessings that we receive when we come here is something completely different. It has so much positivity.

Devotee 25: With each step we take, our negative deeds are nullified. When we come to Matarani, all our wrong deeds, thoughts and negativity are wiped out.

Devotee 26: This temple is more than a thousand years old.

Yogesh Dinkar (priest): In Maharashtra, there are three and a half Shakti peeths and of them the main is Kolhapur.

The places where the trinetra (three eyes) of Sati fell—Mahakali, Mahalakshmi and Mahasaraswati—are taken to be very powerful pilgrim centres. The inner sanctum here is in the shape of the Shree Yantra.

Juhi Chawla: Her divine looks are the path to prosperity; just by glancing at Her potent form one's eyes overflow with devotion. She is the eternal and everlasting strength and force of Kolhapur.

Devotee 27: The Mahalakshmi in Kolhapur is the one who is responsible for the creation of the entire world. She is worshipped under different names—Durga, Padmavati, Mahalakshmi and Amba Mata. In Kolhapur, She is known as Amba Bai.

Juhi Chawla: It is believed that no evil spirit can cross Kolhapur because Ma Amba Bai or Mahalakshmi reigns supreme here.

Devotee 28: A story goes that an angry Ma Amba Bai settled in Kolhapur. In the universe, Brahma, Vishnu and Mahesh all insisted that They were the supreme. There was a sage by the name of Bhrigu, and all three respected him as their spiritual mentor. They invited him to Their homes to take a test. When he went to Kailash, Maheshwar and Parvati were deep in meditation and did not even notice his arrival. This greatly angered Bhrigu and he cursed Shiva that His image would never be worshipped there, but only the symbolic phallic stone.

Juhi Chawla: Next, he went to Brahma, who was in deep conversation with Saraswati. Saraswati was playing the veena (a musical instrument) and Brahma was listening to Her. Both were so engrossed in music that Bhrigu cursed Them too, saying there would be no image of His there and, except in Pushkar, Rajasthan, there would be no temple dedicated to Him.

However, when Bhrigu visited Vishnu, he heard Him telling His wife that Bhrigu would be there any moment to take his test, and that He would answer all his questions and be regarded as the best. 'What! Even before I have taken the exam He is showing off to His wife!' Bhrigu thought. So Bhrigu, angered, planted his feet on Vishnu. The latter, however, reacted by asking him whether he had hurt himself while placing his foot on him. Vishnu then placed Bhrigu on his own seat and sat at his feet.

This, in turn, angered Mahalakshmi and she said, 'You are such a revered God yourself, but when he planted his feet on you, you asked him whether he had been hurt! I have been insulted and will not remain for a moment longer here.' Thus angered, Mahalakshmi returned to Her paternal home in Karveer.

Devotee 29: In Kolhapur, it was the rakshasas, or demons, that predominated.

Devotee 30 (elderly man): There was a demon here by the name of Kalasur, who used to give even the gods a tough time. Then the gods prayed to Mahalakshmi, and She, with Her divine force, destroyed him.

Juhi Chawla: Kalasur then pleaded with Ma that the place of his death be regarded as a pilgrim centre and also the home of Goddess Mahalakshmi. It is from that time that Kolhapur acquired the name it is known by today and Mata Mahalakshmi became the resident goddess of the place. Confronted with the miracles that Ma brings about, people bow their heads in reverence. Wishes are fulfilled without even asking.

Devotee 31: When we enter, there is a floral fragrance around. It makes me feel as though Laxmi Mata is standing right there in front of me. She comes and blesses me.

Devotee 32: I forget my sorrows and problems here. There are only thoughts of Mataji.

Devotee 33: I have epileptic fits and there are two tablets that I have to take for it. But after paying my respects to Ma, even if I do not take the tablets for two consecutive days, I am okay.

Devotee 34: After finishing the sweeping, if there is time, I go inside and pay my respects to Ma. I pray for the welfare of my child and then return. I do this every day.

Devotee 35: My heart pulls me in this direction. I took Her picture home but my steps kept moving in this direction. Ma keeps pulling me here—such a wonderful place this is.

Devotee 36: I come running here. It is so appealing that I do not feel like leaving.

Juhi Chawla: This Shakti peeth is regarded as highly as a moksha peeth. Here, there is the presence of the four-handed Mahalakshmi, Mahakali and Saraswati to bless Their devotees.

Devotee 37: In Kolhapur, each devotee looks upon Mahalakshmi in a different way. All those who worship Her regard Her as Laxmi, to all devotees of Shivji, She is Gauri and for all those who study the Vedas, She is Gayatri. This great and wondrous Mahalakshmi is known in Kolhapur as Amba Bai.

Devotee 38: Our entire lives are taken care of by Her. When I get up in the morning, I take Her name and, at night, before going to sleep, again I take Her name. If there is any work, first I take Her name and then begin.

Devotee 39: The entire year passes by in this manner. We want to go and look upon Her and there is no satisfaction till we have done that.

Devotee 40: When I wake up suddenly at night, sometimes I cannot go back to sleep. Then my daughter-in-law says, 'Ma, you had better sleep, if you don't, Ma Laxmi will also have to stay awake.'

Devotee 41: This is a permanent love, and nobody can change it, neither can one describe it.

Juhi Chawla: Ma—she is the apple of every devotee's eye. Mahalakshmi is the only one in this alien world who is truly our own.

Devotee 42: I have always believed that She is essential to our living. It is my belief that if She is there, everything is there.

Devotee 43 (young man): It is because of Her that we get two square meals a day.

Devotee 44: Any person coming to Kolhapur has never ever had the need to ask Ma for anything. Here, they are blessed with what they want. Travelling all this distance, there is also the belief in people that they have done their duty and now She will do hers.

Juhi Chawla: It is believed that the sins of all who are direct witnesses to Ma's trikaal aarti are laid to rest in the divine court of justice.

Devotee 45: If we witness this aarti ceremony, we consider ourselves lucky to have been at the temple at the right time.

Devotee 46: When I see the Mother's image, it feels like I am being infused with energy.

Devotee 47: I could feel the vibrancy in Her eyes. It seemed like She was my actual mother.

Devotee 48: It feels as though I want to sink into Her eyes and never come out. I just want to stay there, with no memory of home or anybody else. Sitting there, I can only see Her and nobody else.

Juhi Chawla: Every Friday, there is a festival-like atmosphere.

Teeming crowds gather there. The inner link to the divine is thrown open.

Devotee 49: Friday is Ma's day.

Priest: Whoever prays with all sincerity, particularly on a Friday, will have their wishes granted.

Devotee 50: Whatever feelings we have for Ma, we perform with all sincerity—which gives us a lot of peace and serenity. Everything, including anointing Her with vermilion, is done with sincerity.

Juhi Chawla: All through the day, devotees dedicate themselves to the service of the Mother. Every Friday evening, devotees bid farewell to the setting sun. The 600-year-old image of the deity is placed on a throne and taken around the temple. The Mother emerges to bless all Her devotees and becomes part of this unparalleled procession.

Devotee 51: There is a special honour of Mahalakshmi-Amba Bai, and in the palanquin Ma's image is placed; She is the one who emerges to allow devotees to see Her.

Devotee 52: There is an ambience of devotion all around and it feels good to participate in the procession every Friday. Around 5.00 or 6.00 in the evening it is impossible to stay at home—I just have to come to the temple.

Devotee 53: Ma is placed on the palanquin and taken around the premises, stopping at only seven places. Mataji, ensconced on the Garur Throne, enjoys the special services showered on Her by Her devotees. Her devotees sing to Her and offer prayers. For a while there are jubilant celebrations and then a cannon built in 1760 is fired. With this the celebrations come to an end.

Devotee 54: I came here at 4.00 in the morning and have been waiting for the doors to open. I just want to look upon the Goddess. She has filled my heart with joy.

Devotee 55: Whenever I take the name of the Goddess, my eyes brim over. Whenever I take Her name, I feel She is with me. You have come here from somewhere, and so have I. In life, one gets nothing without asking, and so one comes here. Everything depends on belief and there is belief here.

Juhi Chawla: I am ignorant, foolish and in the dark. But whatever I am, I am Your child, and I give You my word that every day I will light a lamp in Your name, and keep it burning. Please continue to bless me.

12

SHANI SHINGNAPUR TEMPLE

A place where faith acquires new meaning and where devotion embarks on a soulful journey, such is the beauty of a peaceful village close to Nashik. Shingnapur is a village where houses have no doors and hearts have no fear. The Shani temple in the village redefines the concept of spirituality and makes you believe in the oneness of the Supreme. Home to several folklores and mythological tales, the Shani Shingnapur temple is the abode of the divine.

Juhi Chawla: When there was nothing, He was omnipresent. When there will be utter emptiness, He will still be there. For aeons, people have an ingrained belief that there is a mystical power that has tied together so many millions of people. Sometimes with hands raised in faith and sometimes with hands folded in obeisance; sometimes carrying thalis of holy offerings, and at others bearing the holy books in faith—through these, all of us are engaged in a continual search for Him.

I, Juhi Chawla, will take you on such a sojourn, which is a unification of all such feelings, which traverses thousands of miles and draws people to the places where we may find Him. The experience of that faith, this journey, is of the conviction that we will.

Devotee 1 (a local): In this village no house has doors. There is never any theft here because God Himself protects this village.

Devotee 2 (man with his family): It is said in this village that if there is any wrongdoing, if someone cheats or steals, he is punished in some way or the other. It instils fear but it is true, because it has actually happened.

Devotee 3 (a local): A thief from some other state had once come here. He stole but then, as he was going out, he got blinded in some way.

Devotee 4: God in reality lives here.

Devotee 5: We go where the deity is, with the faith that our wishes will be fulfilled. That is why people come here.

Devotee 6: Whenever I come here, I express gratitude for all that I have—there is nothing that I have to ask of Him.

Devotee 7: Whatever I want, I tell Him and the work gets done.

Devotee 8 (old man): I believe that whenever God calls, I will come; even if He doesn't, I will go on my own.

Priest: If someone is learning to cycle, he will feel scared. Then someone older will say that there is no need to worry because he will be holding him from the back. So the person gets the courage to cycle. It is the same when people come here; we tell them that we will ask God to hold them and so they begin their journey. All negative thoughts vanish, and they begin to think positively.

Devotee 9: The heart is peaceful and all earthly desires vanish here. When we are in Shingnapur, we are in a different world altogether.

Juhi Chawla: At a distance of about 40 km from Ahmednagar in Gujarat is the village of Shingnapur. The ancient temple of Shani Shingnapur is located here.

Devotee 10: Whenever there is any problem and we call on God Shani with all our hearts, we do not even realize how the problem vanishes. Whether it has been done by God or our fate, I do not really know. But I think it is God who is responsible.

Devotee 11: For me, everything is due to Shani Maharaj. If I am here today, it is only because of Him—there is nothing else but Him.

Devotee 12: I see Shani Bhagwan in my mind and I just have to go to Him; my mind keeps wanting to go back to the temple and pay my respects to Him. Once I do so, I am at peace. My love for Him is overpowering.

Devotee 13: The most potent pilgrim centre is the one where your heart feels at peace. We have been coming to Shingnapur for the past seven years.

Devotee 14: We have been coming here for the past thirty-five years or so.

Devotee 15: I am from Surat, Gujarat.

Devotee 16: I believe in Him so much that I have been coming here for the past fifteen years.

Devotee 17: Every year He draws us here. It is as if something compels us to come—we have to come.

Juhi Chawla: This pilgrim centre is taken as one that is alive, in the sense that God is practically living and breathing here, keeping a vigilant eye so that no evil touches His devotees.

Devotee 18: Throughout India, Shani Shingnapur is known by the name of Shani Maharaj.

Devotee 19 (elderly couple): This is the one and only shrine of Lord Shani.

Devotee 20: Shani Shingnapur is one of the oldest pilgrim centres in India.

Ashok Kulkarni (head priest): A lot of people from Maharashtra and other states come here to pay their respects to the God. Why do they come? Most have some problem or the other with the position of Shani in their natal chart—it is also called 'Sade Sati'. They come here to find a cure to that.

Priest: When we reach the age of twenty–twenty-two, we start preparing for something to achieve—it could be a job or something else. Then the ego takes over—I have achieved so much, studied so much, etc. This ego, or the 'I', is dirt, and that is why Shani Dev starts residing in him for a period of seven and a half years (Sade Sati). At the age of about thirty, the ego fades away. Shani Bhagwan is there only to destroy the ego and nothing else.

Devotee 21: To give you a personal example, we were in a terrible financial crisis. It was like we did not have even a penny to our name. Even in that condition, when we came here, we were told that we were under the influence of the 'Sade Sati' period. Yes, perhaps the Sade Sati period is in my horoscope now. But it is faith—whatever you have taken from me, you will have to repay. We now have a thousand times more than what we have given. The faith is there—it is very difficult to describe.

Everyone wants God to be in their favour and on their side. But people here say, 'Please do not look at my horoscope', because if Shani Bhagwan glances through anyone's horoscope, then the person is sure to face difficult times. However, I say nobody is greater than the person in whose horoscope Shani Dev resides.

Devotee 22: Shani rules the planet Saturn. Some people come here out of reverence, while others do so out of fear.

Juhi Chawla: Shani Dev is one of the most prominent gods in the Hindu religion. The son of Surya (the Sun) and his wife Chhaya, He is counted among those gods who can be potent in making one's life difficult and full of problems, but He is also one of the greatest well-wishers and gods to help His devotees.

Devotee 23: Whenever we stand in front of a judge, irrespective of whether we are guilty, our heart quakes. Shani Dev is the God of Justice. When it is His turn to take a stance, i.e. in the Sade Sati period, He makes us account for all that we have done in the period.

Devotee 24: If you have done wrong or been unfair, you are bound to be afraid—you will be punished. And if you have done good, you will be rewarded.

Family of devotees: Shani Dev does give a host of problems and difficulties, but when He leaves, He leaves with a plethora of gifts.

Juhi Chawla: Here, Shani Bhagwan is in the shape of a luminescent black rock, beneath the open skies, ensconced in a reservoir. But the temple has no pattern or roof. This form of Shaniji is a self-evolved image, which means it was not constructed by man but created by the forces of nature.

Devotee 25: Shani Dev has evolved in this form by Himself. Nobody has brought it forth, but it is said that it evolved at this spot.

Juhi Chawla: There is an incident that happened 350–400 years ago. There was torrential downpour in Shingnapur village. It rained so hard that it seemed there was going to be a flood. Finally, when it stopped raining and the floodwaters receded, the herdsmen stepped out to feed the cows, and that is when they saw lying next to an uprooted tree the huge black granite-like stone.

Devotee 26 (a local): One of the herdsmen jabbed at it with a stick and it started oozing blood. They talked of this to the elders of the village and everybody gathered there.

Devotee 27: But when they tried to move the stone, nothing happened. It remained immobile. Everyone got worried. That night a farmer had a dream.

Juhi Chawla: God Shaneswar Himself appeared in His dream and said that the black stone was His self-evolved form. He also said that His rock would move only with the joint efforts of mama-bhanja, or uncle and nephew. The rock was to be picked up and taken to the village and established there.

Devotee 28: The villagers tried to lift Him but couldn't.

Devotee 29: Then they understood that He did not want to be brought to the village in this manner; He would have to be pulled in a bullock cart. The bullocks, along with the humans, were mama-bhanja. When they were passing the point where Shani Dev is now established, He refused to budge.

Juhi Chawla: Since that day Shani Bhagwan is instated in an open space, without any roof.

Devotee 30: There is always an inner sanctum (garbha griha) for the God. Here, for Shani Dev, the firmament is his roof and creation is his inner sanctum.

Devotee 31: The shade of the surrounding neem trees do not fall upon the Shani rock, as Shani Bhagwan wants to live without any shade over Him.

Devotee 32: A branch from a nearby tree was growing towards the Shani rock but every time it would come close, it would break off by itself. Initially, there were a few villagers who worshipped the stone, but then the number gradually grew. People made offerings but nothing got done. Then Shani Bhagwan let it be known that He was the child of the Sun and should be left in the open. So, despite a lot of efforts, there is no temple there.

Juhi Chawla: No matter if it is cold, hot or rainy, twenty-four hours Shani Dev is always ready to bless His followers. The presence of Shani Dev in the form of the black stone creates a mesmerizing ambience.

Devotee 33: I have served God for three months here. I am living on the fruits of that service even now. It is impossible for me to believe that sorrow will never come to me. My only prayer is that if I am ever reborn as a human, please let me be able to serve Shani Dev right from the beginning.

Devotee 34: Just as when we fall down and involuntarily cry out for our mother and she comes to help us up, similarly Shani Dev immediately hears our problem and takes care of us.

Devotee 35: No matter what we do in life, some sort of moral support is needed. That we get here.

Juhi Chawla: In the temple dedicated to Shani Shingnapur, at least 30,000 devotes stand in queue to worship Him every day. Everyone who comes here, in their dedication and devotion makes earnest efforts to understand Him and seek His blessings.

Devotee 36: Of all the gods, we are most attached to Shani Dev. My husband and I make plans to come here every few months.

Devotee 37 (middle-aged man): I love Shani Bhagwan. He is with me all the time. Whenever I am in any kind of problem, it seems help is bound to come in the form of Shani Dev.

Devotee 38: God is not seen but His presence can always be felt inside.

Devotee 39: Every Saturday I come here—not to ask for anything but just to see Him.

Devotee 40: I worship Him because I fear Him. At the same time, when I give Him my offerings, there is a sense of happiness and gratitude, and I try to give what I can to make Him happy.

Juhi Chawla: It is tradition to worship Shani Bhagwan with black sesame and mustard oil. There is a description of how this started in tales from the Puranas. It says in the Ramayana that one day Hanumanji was sitting under a tree and concentrating on Guru Sri Ram. All of a sudden, Shani Bhagwan appeared before Him and, with great ferocity, flaunted His strength and began making unreasonable demands. Hanumanji replied that He was concentrating on Ram and would not like to be disturbed. But Shani Dev was not willing to listen. Hanumanji then coiled His tail around Him very tightly. And try as He may, Shani Bhagwan could not free Himself. When the pain became unbearable, He begged for forgiveness from Hanumanji for His ego. Only then was He freed. When Shani Bhagwan asked Hanumanji by what means the pain could be lessened, He was advised to apply mustard oil.

Priest: Since then, it has been the norm. Legend has it that Shani Bhagwan Himself said, 'Whenever the stars are in a troublesome constellation—such as Sade Sati—anoint me with mustard and black sesame oil. This will lessen the agony to a large extent.' The best day to do this is on a Saturday, which is the day dedicated to Shani Bhagwan. If at the time of sunrise, a peepal tree is bathed in mustard oil and black sesame oil, Shani Bhagwan will shower His blessings on them.

Devotee 41: I used to take ten minutes to climb ten stairs—I poured mustard oil on Shani Maharaj and after that, everything was all right.

Devotee 42: I used to run a hospital and was then faced with a severe financial crisis. I started brooding. The situation was such that anyone else in my position would have thought of committing suicide. Then I prayed to Shani Maharaj, and things are better now.

Devotee 43: People are scared and advise others to stay away from Shani Dev, but He is the one to depend on in this Kalyug.

Devotee 44: There is a tradition that from the month of Sravana (rainy season), the villagers can ascend the platform and anoint Him with water.

Devotee 45 (a local): This rainy season is believed to be very holy and every single day is auspicious. That is why during this period, thousands of devotees throng the place and anoint Him with mustard oil, seeking His blessings and praying to Him to solve their problems.

Devotee 46: Normally the tradition of pouring oil happens only in the month of Sravana (Saturdays of the month). That is why my entire family comes here at the time.

Devotee 47: All devotees can access Shani Dev through the Shani rock—it is because you are not allowed to look directly at Shani Bhagwan's eyes. So here we have the opportunity of coming to Him and approaching Him, touching Him and receiving His blessings.

Juhi Chawla: In order to please Shani Bhagwan, He is adorned and worshipped in a princely fashion, and His name is chanted and honoured a number of times. Some incantations are extremely difficult, while others are fairly easy. But it is vital to remember that what we regard as the most tough time is also the most beneficial, because this is the time when the soul matures. It is Shani Bhagwan who is responsible for this in everyone's lives at some point of time or the other.

13

MAA BHADRAKALI DEVIKOOP

Kurukshetra in Haryana, a place of immense historical and mythological importance, boasts one of the most powerful Shakti peeths in India—Maa Bhadrakali Devikoop Temple. Hailed as the sacred place where Mata Sati's right ankle fell, Maa Bhadrakali Devikoop temple receives thousands of visitors every year. Legend has it that before marching out for the Kurukshetra battle, the Pandavas, along with Lord Krishna, prayed here for their victory and donated their horses, which started an age-old tradition of devotees offering horses made of silver, mud, etc. A sense of solace and peace reigns around Maa Bhadrakali Temple. The comfort of a mother's lap and the assurance that nothing can go wrong when one is devoted to Maa Bhadrakali is what drives ardent followers to this serene locale.

Juhi Chawla: When there was nothing, He was omnipresent. When there will be utter emptiness, He will still be there. For aeons, people have an ingrained belief that there is a mystical power that has tied together so many millions of people. Sometimes with hands raised in faith and sometimes with hands folded in obeisance; sometimes carrying thalis of holy offerings, and at others bearing the holy books in faith—through these, all of us are engaged in a continual search for Him.

I, Juhi Chawla, will take you on such a sojourn, which is a unification of all such feelings, which traverses thousands of miles and draws people to the places where we may find Him. The experience of that faith, this journey, is of the conviction that we will.

Devotee 1: I cannot describe what this place means to me, how much She gives. She is bountiful.

Devotee 2: At home I keep crying. But that stops when I enter the temple gates. My family scoff and say that I am play-acting. But the Mother knows.

Juhi Chawla: The first word we utter after birth is 'Ma'. It is also the last word when we die. My pilgrim centre is your lap, O Mother. Kailash is where You are.

Devotee 3: All that I ask from Mother is that I am able to serve Her all my life—may I always be at Her revered feet. That as long as there is breath in my body, may I be able to be of service to Her.

Devotee 4: If I am unable to come even one day, it becomes difficult for me. Just like a child becomes desperate for its mother, I become desperate when I cannot come here. If there are problems, sorrows or difficulties, we sit near Ma and She listens to everything.

Devotee 5: Come with faith and ask for whatever you want. You will leave with everything you wanted and will be singing her praises—'Jai Mata Di!'

Juhi Chawla: It is believed that even if the dust of the hallowed Kurukshetra touches you, your sins will be washed away.

The most remarkable thing about Kurukshetra is that whether on land, water or air—wherever death occurs in Kurukshetra—you go straight to Brahmalok (Heaven). This is the arena of Dharmakshetra, where Sri Krishna gave the advice that now constitutes the Bhagavad Gita. It is the place where the Battle of Kurukshetra was fought.

Devotee 6 (a local): When the battle of Mahabharata took place, this was the place where Lord Sri Krishna prayed for the strength of the Pandavas and also their victory. Kurukshetra is worshipped because the Mother is the resident deity there.

Juhi Chawla: About 1,500 km from Delhi, in Haryana, is Kurukshetra—which is the prime centre of worship for Ma Shakti. Dedicated here is a temple to the Goddess Ma Bhadrakali Devi.

Devotee 7: When we come to the temple and pay our respects to the Mother, our hearts seem to become calm. There is great satisfaction on meeting the Mother.

Devotee 8 (middle-aged man): There is peace after coming here; all worries and concerns go away.

Devotee 9 (young boy): There is a different kind of energy here, a positive and magnetic feeling, which is why people throng here.

Devotee 10: Coming to the temple, belief and devotion increases; there comes a time when no negative thoughts enter your mind. Gradually this becomes a habit and there is never any negative thought in your mind. No matter how many times you come to the temple, you take back something positive.

Devotee 11: I am from Panipat and have been coming here for the past ten years.

Devotee 12: I have been coming to pay my respects to Ma for the past twenty–twenty-five years.

Devotee 13: I have been coming here for eleven years now. It is Ma's will—as long as She brings me here, I will come. It is my wish that I breathe my last here.

Devotee 14: Whenever someone stands before the image of a deity and talks about his or her own self, it is done with the belief that someone is listening. Thanks to that belief, if something you wanted is fulfilled, the belief grows that someone is indeed listening. And that is the person to talk to.

Devotee 15: About a year ago, there were a lot of ups and downs in my life. I was frustrated. There was no friend to talk to and neither could I converse with my family. At that time a temple seemed to be the only place I could go to and unburden my issues. It seemed to me that She was listening and would do something for me; I had asked for two or three things, and they were all fulfilled. That is why I have come here to pay my respects.

Juhi Chawla: The place where millions come to offer their respects has been trodden by Sati Ma herself. The Bhadrakali

Temple is an ancient pilgrim centre (Shakti peeth). Here fell Ma Sati's right leg, cut by Lord Vishnu's Sudarshan Chakra. That is why this temple is known as Devi ka Koop—the well of the Devi.

Satpal Sharma (head priest): The Devi Bhadrakali Temple is one of the fifty-two Shakti peeths of Ma Sati and Ma Bhadrakali. She is the mighty force that regulates time, who is known as Kali. Descriptions are also available for Her—Chamunda Kali, Guhya Kali, Ugra Kali, Rudra Kali, Dakshina Kali, Maha Kali and Shamshan Kali. Here, Ma takes the form of Bhadra Kali.

Juhi Chawla: 'Bha' means illusion or maya, and 'dra' means the harbinger of greatness. So, the meaning of 'bhadra' stands as 'the Mighty Illusion'. She is the one who empathizes with Her devotees. Ma Bhadrakali is actually Parvati, the wife of Lord Shiva. She was created to destroy the demons and save the gods.

Satpal Sharma: To help the Goddess, all the gods bestowed on Her a unique weapon each. It was in this person that Ma destroyed the demons. After the killing, She became almost uncontrollable and even started wielding the weapons against the gods. So the gods pleaded with Shankar Bhagwan (Shiva) to stop this destruction.

Devotee 16: So, Shankar Bhagwan broke His meditation and lay down in Ma's path of destruction. Ma inadvertently stepped on Him, with Her right foot on His chest.

Satpal Sharma: Shankar Bhagwan played on the small hourglass drum he carries. This brought Ma to Her senses and She realized that She had stepped on none other than Shankar Bhagwan Himself. She immediately realized Her mistake and stepped back.

Devotee 17: Since then She has been known as Bhadra Kali.

Satpal Sharma: So here one gets to see the tranquil form of Ma.

Juhi Chawla: Ma Kali, who terrifies the demons, is to Her devotees the veritable image of compassion and kindness.

Devotee 18: Whenever I close my eyes, I only see Her face and nothing else.

Devotee 19: I have such deep and abiding love for Ma. She is, after all, our fundamental strength.

Devotee 20: She is the mother of love. Those who approach Her with true belief will be shown the path of heaven.

Devotee 21: At the temple of Ma Bhadra Kali one can forget all sorrows and problems.

Juhi Chawla: Ma, only Your blessings help me. You fill my emptiness and do everything possible for me. If I raise my hands, You are the firmament and if I lower my head, You are the very Mother Earth.

Devotee 22: There is no sorrow if one bows before Ma and talks to Her of all troubles. It feels like nectar.

Devotee 23: It is heavenly at the Mother's feet. She is the mother of all creation.

Devotee 24: The entire universe is at Her feet. Anything that is sought with confidence and reverence is always granted.

Devotee 25: Even if I have pleaded with Ma for something unjustified, I have got it. You will be amazed at all the miracles that have happened in my life.

Devotee 26: It seems to me that I have actually found my birth mother here. I have found a lot of peace here. There has been a lot of prosperity for my entire family too. My husband is a Class VIII fail, but Ma made him into a thriving contractor.

Devotee 27: I have got everything from here. Whatever I have wanted has been given to me. I wanted children, I got them. When I go to say anything, my heart overflows and I find it difficult to express myself.

Devotee 28: Ma has given me so much love that no one else will ever be able to give me...

Juhi Chawla: One who has lit the light of devotion at Ma's threshold can be sure that it will never go out, no matter how strong the wind is. In the Mahabharata, it is mentioned that the Pandavas had sat here with Sri Krishna and sought the blessings of Goddess Durga. After attaining victory, they came once again to the same temple and, in gratitude, made the offering of a horse. Ever since, this has been a tradition. Devotees bow in obeisance to the ever-burning light and, once their plea is fulfilled, according to their abilities and desires, make an offering of a clay, silver or gold miniature horse/horses.

Devotee 29: According to what is possible and what the means are, people make offerings of silver, gold or clay horses in miniature. It is only after the desire or wish is fulfilled that the offering is made.

Devotee 30: We had suddenly been confronted with a major problem, which was service-related. Ma put an end to all our problems and we made an offering of silver horses—now my daughter has got a job and the day she joins, I will make another offering.

Devotee 31: We had no house, and I had promised Ma that the day we have our own home, I would come and make an offering of a silver horse. Ma answered our prayers, even though we had nothing. My husband had a very simple job with the government. But I cannot express how much Ma gave us—so to fulfil our promise, we made the offering.

Juhi Chawla: The desires and wishes of millions of people are fulfilled by Ma. No matter how far Her devotees are, Ma draws them close and fulfils their emptiness.

Devotee 32 (middle-aged lady): All this while we have been coming because of Her kindness, and in the future too, if we are able to come, it will be because of Her kindness. It is not in our power to come without Her calling. If She is kind enough, we will come.

Devotee 33: We take one step and Ma calls to us. That is how She enthuses us, and we are able to come to the temple—we would not have been able to do so otherwise.

Devotee 34: When I enter the temple, I forget everything about the make-believe world. This temple means more than heaven to me.

Juhi Chawla: The ambience of the temple remains luminescent every single day. But Saturdays in particular are special here. A variety of floral decorations are seen everywhere. There are lights in every corner. Devotees throng the temple as though it were a wedding they were attending. There are hymns being sung and music being played in the courtyard. Seeing all these joyous devotees, it seems that someone has smeared the entire atmosphere with vermilion.

Devotee 35: It is believed that Ma is the most powerful on Saturdays.

Devotee 36: Matarani appears in all her power on this day; She appears before us in Her entirety.

Devotee 37: When I look upon Her, my eyes brim over.

Devotee 38: When that force is awakened in the devotees, they dance, sing with joy. Ma puts that joyful spirit in them.

Juhi Chawla: Each Saturday there is a langar (free meals for everyone). But prior to that, nine young girls (kanyas) are worshipped and anointed. These nine girls are taken to be the nine divine forms of Goddess Durga. After that, all devotees partake of the langar.

Devotee 39: Every Saturday a bhandara or langar takes place at the Bhadrakali temple. Every day we have our meals at home. However, if on a Saturday we get the chance to have a meal with Ma, it is our good fortune.

Devotee 40: If we get to have the blessed food, it is like nectar for us. This cannot be compared to anything else. You could get peace of mind after partaking of the blessed food, or if you are suffering from any medical problem—it is the frame of mind in which you are eating that matters. Ma will definitely give you what you are seeking.

Devotee 41 (a couple): As the saying goes, as you think and partake of the food, so shall the results be. The results will be in accordance with the manner in which you partake of this blessed food.

Devotee 42: This blessed food has a lot of strength in it. Any being, any human, anybody who eats this becomes part of Ma themselves.

Juhi Chawla: It is believed that anyone who eats this food, which has already been tasted by the Mother, remains forever blessed with good fortune. This staunch devotion is what keeps the faith alive in Her devotees.

Devotee 43: I was ill, and the doctor had given me an injection. I was lying on a charpoy, and She came and stood right beside me. I told my husband that Ma was there, and he asked me if I could feel Her presence. I replied that I could see Her. I asked him to just close his eyes and focus on Her.

Devotee 44: I get up in the morning and think of Her. Whenever there is any kind of activity, whether it is the naming ceremony of a child or any kind of purchase, Her name is always taken.

Juhi Chawla: The more you intensify your devotion to the temple, the more your life will shine. If a lamp is lit at Ma's feet, She will ensure that all the darkness in your life vanishes.

There are a number of worshipping ceremonies throughout the day, but the evening ceremony has a special significance. The sound of conch shells resounds in the temple. Time itself seems to stand still when devotees praise Ma as loudly as they can. There is unwavering faith among the devotees that during the time of this ceremony, Ma is alive and among all of them.

Devotee 45: The vibrations make the heart tremble. It feels like Ma is inside us. At that time, our hearts overflow with joy.

Devotee 46: At the time of the aarti, all attention is focused on Ma. After the aarti, it feels as though we are light and carefree. There is no tension at all.

Devotee 47: You look at the image of the Goddess and your problems are resolved then and there. Ma is hungry only for true devotion.

Devotee 48: For me, Ma means more than my own life.

Devotee 49: I cannot express in words the miracles I have seen Ma working. In me, there is a lot of feeling and emotion about Her.

Devotee 50: Ma is not the one to give medicines, all She bestows on you is love.

Juhi Chawla: Belief is the true path of faith. That is a form that truly ignites life. In belief and devotion there can only be love. This love is what makes life joyous and beautiful. Belief and faith can make an unfeeling stone come alive. It constitutes everything.

14

BRAHMA TEMPLE

In Pushkar, Rajasthan, lies one of the oldest temples, dedicated to Lord Brahma, the creator of the universe and everything within it. Thousands of devotees throng the temple and the adjoining Pushkar Sarovar to seek blessings. Discover the mystic energy that draws people to this holy site in this chapter.

Juhi Chawla: When there was nothing, He was omnipresent. When there will be utter emptiness, He will still be there. For aeons, people have an ingrained belief that there is a mystical power that has tied together so many millions of people. Sometimes with hands raised in faith and sometimes with hands folded in obeisance; sometimes carrying thalis of holy offerings, and at others bearing the holy books in faith—through these, all of us are engaged in a continual search for Him.

I, Juhi Chawla, will take you on such a sojourn, which is a unification of all such feelings, which traverses thousands of miles and draws people to the places where we may find Him. The experience of that faith, this journey, is of the conviction that we will.

In the firmament of empathy and understanding dawned devotion. There was no worry about life and neither did death rear its head. It is the Almighty who grasped the reins.

Ascetic: I pray to the Almighty to make me meet my death here at this place.

Devotee 1: This is what I live and die for.

Devotee 2 (elderly couple): My wife has a problem with walking, and tends to drag her feet. But she insists on coming here; the Lord's image drags us here.

Devotee 3: There is a kind of peace here. It feels like we are in a nice place, and the heart is induced into feeling and doing good.

Devotee 4 (ascetic in saffron): There is a great feeling of joy when His name is taken.

Devotee 5: He is the father and will give to all. Whoever comes will receive. He will give according to the deeds that have been done.

Juhi Chawla: About 16 km from Ajmer, in Rajasthan, is Pushkar. For centuries, it has been situated among the Aravalli hills, alongside the Pushkar Sarovar, a small reservoir.

Devotee 6: If a person visits the four dhams, or main pilgrim centres, but does not bathe in Pushkar, his pilgrimage is futile. This is regarded as the guru of all pilgrim sites.

Devotee 7: Just as the primary worship spot for Vishnu is Gaya in Bihar and for Shiva is Kasi-Varanasi, for Brahma it is Pushkar. 'Pushp' means flower and 'kar' means the hand of Brahma.

Juhi Chawla: It is believed that Brahma Himself created Pushkar and all the mysticism around it.

Devotee 8: The resting place of Lord Vishnu is Shirsagar. From his navel the lotus flower sprouts, which is where Brahmaji was born. He then tells Vishnu that now that He had been born, He wanted a pilgrim centre of His own. So Vishnuji said, 'Brahmaji, you were born on a lotus—take this lotus and go to Brahmalok and from there cast down the flower.'

Ascetic: Vishnu asked Brahma to perform a ceremonial worship where the flower fell. Pushkar was where the flower fell, and because the earth was struck, water gushed out.

Juhi Chawla: Brahma was born and thus creation, or srishti, took place. Every place the lotus touched became fragrant. The reservoir created in the middle of Pushkar Dham was replete with an ambience of devotion, steering everybody to its shores. The very air around inspires a different kind of sensation. In this place, even the high and mighty bow their heads in reverence.

Devotee 9 (local man): If anyone is to truly savour the mysticism of this place, one has to come here and choose any corner of the ghat and, whether in the morning or evening, sit there and focus. He or she will feel such a mystical sense of joy. In the peace and solitude of the waters here, there is a strange kind of strength, which can be felt only by those who come here. To imbibe this sensation, people from all over the world visit Pushkar.

Devotee 10: My name is Shana and I am originally from America; I reached Pushkar only last week. But four months earlier, I had taken off and was here for five months straight.

Devotee 11: I have come from a far-off place.

Ascetic in saffron: I have been coming here since 1984.

Juhi Chawla: This is the place Sri Ram came to perform the obsequies of His mother and father, the place where bathing in the sarovar, the entire being changes, becomes unique. A person who comes here even for the first time feels that this is where he belongs.

Devotee 12 (a man who visits regularly): Meditating near Pushkar, singing holy songs or giving alms only happens if it is destined for you. In the Satyug (Era of Truth) there was no other pilgrimage but Pushkar...and in the Treta Yug it was Kurukshetra. In the Kalyug it is the Ganga, which was brought by Bhagirath... There are five holy sarovars—the Brahma Sarovar, the Manas Sarovar, the Bindu Sarovar, the Pampa Sarovar and the Narayan Sarovar.

Juhi Chawla: It is said that if you if you take a dip in the sarovar and don't know how to swim, if you get to the other side, it is faith and if you drown, it is freedom.

Devotee 13: Even if you sit near the Pushkar Sarovar for only five minutes, you will feel close to heaven. To give alms here, to meditate and organize ceremonies enhances all positive results.

Devotee 14: The water of the Pushkar Sarovar is auspicious. Lord Shiva once admonished Brahma for demonstrating incestuous behaviour and cut off his fifth head for this 'unholy' behaviour. Since Brahma had distracted His mind from the soul and towards the cravings of the flesh, Lord Shiva's curse was that people should not worship Brahma. And hence it is said that the temple of Brahmaji is cursed. This is the only Brahma temple in the world. The sarovar is potent—all our sorrows and problems are resolved here.

Devotee 15: The water of this sarovar is very holy. We carry it home in a container. We have a temple and it is used there. We also use it at home to drink and for making dough.

Devotee 16: Bathing in this water cures ills and leads to a sense of fulfilment. According to the lunar calendar, in the month of Kartika, from the day after the New Moon till the Full Moon, for five days, millions of people bathe here and pray for the eternal peace of their forefathers. Pushkar is known as the eternal and everlasting pilgrimage.

Ascetic in saffron: It was 1984. When I was going there at 4 o'clock in the morning to bathe, people from a Naga sect cut a tuft of hair on my head beneath the tree. When the tuft of hair was cut, I discarded all my clothes (except the loin cloth) and went for a bath at Brahm Ghat. Then Brahmaji in His four forms revealed Himself to me.

Juhi Chawla: Pushkar Dham is firmly ensconced in the hearts of devotees. They bow respectfully before the Creator, Brahma. He is all-powerful and from Him stems true faith and belief. Pushkar Dham is such a pillar on which the firmament rests. It is believed that when you step out after a bath in the sarovar, you smell of lotuses. They say all paths will lead to the Pushkar temple, where Brahmaji Himself resides.

Devotee couple: We go there to look upon Him, and gazing at His face, we are fulfilled.

Devotee 17: There is a belief that even if someone's feet have blisters and they are unable to walk properly, Brahmaji ensures that they are able to reach.

Devotee 18: I have received a lot from here. I had prayed that I get into NIIT—and now I have got admission into NIIT Patna.

Devotee 19 (young couple): We had come here a year ago to pray for a girl; now we have a girl child and have returned to offer our prayers again.

Juhi Chawla: The Brahma Temple is the only sacred place where Brahma is worshipped. Devotees from all over the world come here. Joining both palms together they gaze at Brahmaji.

Devotee 20: Looking at Him I feel relaxed and tension-free. It seems that He is standing right in front of me, listening to me. There is so much peace here.

Devotee 21: Pushkar is the reigning monarch of all pilgrim centres. That is why He is known as Pushkar Raj.

Holy man in saffron: It is believed that Brahmaji is the Creator of the universe. Whatever people see around is all His creation, Brahma Srishti.

Devotee 22: Brahmaji is the guru (spiritual mentor)—there can be no true knowledge without Him, there can be no freedom without Him. Brahmaji is the father of the world.

Devotee 23: The place of the mentor is inviolable. Nobody can lessen His stature in my eyes. There is a lot of love for Him.

Juhi Chawla: Brahma is the Creator. But He cannot be worshipped in any other place but Pushkar.

A group of devotees: Brahmaji Himself meditated here for 10,000 years, after which He got his own auspicious astronomical time—Karthik Shukla Ekadashi to Poornima. This is the mahurat on which the Pushkar fair has been organized for ages.

Devotee 24: In our religious texts it is clearly stated that no religious ceremony will be fulfilled if both husband and wife are not present.

Ascetic: Brahma's wife is Savitri. Once, Brahma sent for Narad and asked Him to escort Her. The thought then occurred to Him that He had seen everyone in the world fighting but not His parents. 'If I am unable to get my parents to fight, then who will acknowledge me as Narad?'

So He said to Savitri, 'So many people mill around Brahmaji—monarchs, kings and queens, dressed in such gorgeous attire. It does not look good if you go there in this fashion—it is belittling to your status.'

After this, Narad went to Brahma and said, 'Mother is bathing and will take some time to arrive.' As Savitri got further delayed and the auspicious moment was almost over, Brahma was incensed and immediately ordered Indra: 'Go and find any girl you can and bring her here. I will marry her and proceed with the ceremony.' By wile Indra picked up a girl and brought her there. All the sages and holy men protested that she was of a low caste and could get married to Him. The only way out was for her to be extracted from a cow so she is regarded as Brahmin. Certain spells were cast and a Kamdhenu cow was brought (Kamdhenu is a cow that can produce milk without bearing a calf), and by the same mystical means the woman was extracted from its back thrice. She was named Gayatri.

The Gayatri Mantra or incantation is believed to be her point of evolvement.

Gayatriji was thus married to Brahma. When the ceremony was partially completed, Savitri arrived. She saw this new woman sitting beside Brahmaji and the wedding ceremony being carried out, in which all the gods were participating. Savitri was enraged, and Brahmaji was the first to be cursed. 'Nowhere in the world will there be any temple dedicated to you,' She told Him. Hence, Brahma is worshipped only here in Pushkar.

Juhi Chawla: The concepts and points of view might well be different, but the thread of belief keeps everyone knit together. Devotion keeps an unclothed body well covered.

Devotee couple: Our day starts with Brahmaji's blessed food (prasad) and then we have breakfast. We take just a bit and before it finishes come here.

Devotee 25 (a local): I am prospering because of Brahmaji's kindness.

Devotee 26: There was some problem about land and property. I gave my word to Brahmaji that if my problem was resolved, I would keep certain promises I was making. The problem has now been taken care of.

Devotee 27: We are like His children and He is the father. If we have problems, He will surely understand all that is troubling us. Brahmaji is a father and guru. There is no need to ask for anything—a father knows the needs of his children and takes care of them.

Juhi Chawla: When Savitri cursed Brahmaji, in volatile anger, She merged into the western mountain range of Ratnagiri. Even today, devotees go to the temple there to pay their respects to Savitriji.

Devotee 28: Brahma had ignored Savitri at the time of a special ceremony. So in anger She merged into these mountains.

Devotee 29 (young man): If you do not go to Savitri Ma after you go to Brahmaji, your visit will be futile.

Devotee 30: Savitri Ma gives one blessings for a long married life—which is why there are a lot of visitors there. I had fallen in love with a girl once and had come here with her. I begged Savitri Ma that She get us married. I do not know what happened, but all of a sudden our engagement was fixed about one and a half months later, and we got married.

Juhi Chawla: No matter how diverse their strengths and how deep the discord between the deities, there is never any negative influence on the devotees. True faith is always acknowledged.

There is so much love in the atmosphere at Pushkar that devotees are mesmerized. In the stories that are narrated about them, there is only positivity.

Devotee 31 (chanting Om Sri Brahmaye Namah Devaye Namah): Every art form is divine. Before starting on any, one has to pray to God and the guru. If true prayers anoint art, it adds a different dimension to it. The Vedas and the Puranas mention Brahma as having four faces—He is shown sporting a gold locket and a bejewelled crown, and has a white beard.

I never had anything and I don't have anything now either. It was Brahmaji who wanted me to work here, and so He made arrangements. This is the power of God—it is His strength that creates it all. There is no artist who would otherwise have any capacity to do anything. This is the blessing of God and that is with which I am working. This Brahmand (the Universe), this is it.

Devotee 32: We have two showrooms—one upstairs and one below that. It is because of His kindness that all this was possible.

Devotee 33 (a young cycle-rickshaw driver): Whenever I stand in the market, I remember Him and beg Him to do something for me. Almost immediately I get a passenger.

Juhi Chawla: It is You we talk about; it is You we remember. Please always be with us in this manner. You are the night, you are the day.

Ascetic in saffron: *Jai Pushkar Raj Ki… Jai Pushkar Raj Ki… Jai Pushkar Raj Ki!*

15

HAZUR SAHIB

The sands of time often stand witness to the events that take place around them. Nanded, a peaceful town set close to the city of Aurangabad in Maharashtra, stands testament to the magical aura of the legendary Guru Gobind Singh. With an air of divinity around it, Nanded is home to the fourth seat of Sikhism—Hazur Sahib, a gurudwara where it is widely believed that Guru Gobind Singh stayed and gave his last sermon from.

Juhi Chawla: When there was nothing, He was omnipresent. When there will be utter emptiness, He will still be there. For aeons, people have an ingrained belief that there is a mystical power that has tied together so many millions of people. Sometimes with hands raised in faith and sometimes with hands folded in obeisance; sometimes carrying thalis of holy offerings, and at others bearing the holy books in faith—through these, all of us are engaged in a continual search for Him.

I, Juhi Chawla, will take you on such a sojourn, which is a unification of all such feelings, which traverses thousands of miles and draws people to the places where we may find Him. The experience of that faith, this journey, is of the conviction that we will.

No problems can beset a person who has a true bonding with the Almighty. These words are those of the first Sikh Guru—Guru Nanak. Keeping this belief in the Guru firm, every year millions of devotees come to Nanded and submit their desires at the feet of the Guru.

Devotee 1: A true Sikh is one who has learnt the Eternal Truth and followed the path of the Guru.

Devotee 2: One who follows the teaching of the Guru is a real Sikh. According to the Guruvani, the Guru has come to liberate us from the cycle of birth and death. And as such, it is our duty to give something back to him, to follow him.

Devotee 3: Just like the wire that brings us electricity, there is a wire connecting us with Guruji.

Devotee 4: Our Guru is the greatest for us and life remains unfulfilled without him. He is the one who shows us the path.

Devotee 5: It's the Guru who will show us the path ahead. That is why we feel it's necessary to visit our Guru.

Devotee 6: It's just like how a patient needs a hospital—it is impossible to be treated at home. We come, are treated and then we return home after getting better. That is why we come to this gurudwara. Guru Maharaj is a doctor for us, who knows everything about us.

Juhi Chawla: At a distance of about 275 km from Aurangabad in Maharashtra, moving south from the Ganga, on the banks of the holy Godavari, is situated Nanded. No sooner does one step here than it seems that one has reached the threshold of the Guru. Of them, one renowned 'dwar' is Sri Hazur Afzal Nagar Sahib Gurudwara.

Devotee 7: The first time I visited the gurudwara, I had no emotion—I froze. Then I was like, 'Wow! Why did it actually take me so long to come here? How have I missed this all this while?'

Juhi Chawla: Sri Hazur Afzal Nagar Sahib Gurudwara is one of the most holy centres of the Sikh faith. This gurudwara is also known as Sachkhand, which means 'a place of truth'. In reality, this can only be possible where the Almighty Himself resides.

Devotee 8: People believe that when they die they go to heaven. But for us, this is our virtual heaven.

Devotee 9: There is something magical and mystical here, a certain spirituality. The greatness of this place cannot be described in words. It has to be felt by coming here.

Devotee 10: Each moment is wonderful here. On reaching this place, a person forgets everything else, and is just mindful of their connection to God.

Devotee 11: One can feel the presence of the Almighty here.

Devotee 12: Every single moment, as long as we are here, the only thoughts in our mind are of God.

Jagbir Singh (head kathavachak in Hazur Sahib): All Sikhs are aware of the fact that Guru Sahibji had gone towards Nanded, towards the South. So when the Sikh community comes here to pay its respects to the Guru, when asked where they are going, the answer is, 'We are going to the Hazuri of Hazur.' Since the advent of Guru Gobind Sahibji, this place has come to be known as Hazur Sahib.

Devotee 13 (elderly man): On coming here I feel a lot of peace. This is the house of the Lord.

Devotee 14: There are always two aspects to any person—the positive and the negative. After coming here, everything negative goes away and only the positive remains.

Devotee 15: Our ego is shattered here. There is a different kind of feeling when one comes here.

Devotee 16: Any filth in the heart is cleansed when one comes here. The only thought that stays is, 'We will leave behind all that is ugly and take back only the good.'

Juhi Chawla: Here, there is a constant feeling of the presence of the Almighty. In every corner of this hallowed ground, there is the presence of a mighty warrior like Guru Gobind Singh, the holy words he uttered and his love and empathy for all.

Devotee 17: It is God who has brought me so far. I had to come here because of Him. There is God in my heart and at home, so there is no question of going anywhere to find Him, but when I come here, I realize what this place is. God is above everything and everybody else, and that is why we have to come here.

Devotee 18: About eighteen–twenty of us have come from Bhilai.

Devotee 19 (elderly man): For the past fifteen years, we have been coming here every year.

Devotee 20: I have come here for Shukrani Ardas, or thanksgiving prayers, with my family.

Devotee 21: There is nothing like the peace that is found here. I cannot put into words what I get here. I do not feel like going back to the outside world after coming here. I do not want to leave this place at all.

Juhi Chawla: It is impossible to describe the ambience of this place—it can only be felt. This gurudwara was built at the site where Guru Gobind Singh died. The interiors of the gurudwara are known as the Angithasahib. It is built on the exact spot where the obsequies of Guru Gobind Singh were carried out in 1708. This is the spot where Sri Sahib Singh Guru Maharaj attained heaven.

The Angithasahib was where all the rites took place, and the common man is forbidden to go there. This is also that momentous place where on 7 October 1708, a few days before his demise, Guru Gobind Singh made a momentous announcement in his last sermon—that no Sikh was to worship any human form, just the Guru Granth Sahib.

Foreign devotee: The light, the spirit of the temple was put into the Guru Granth Sahib by Guru Gobind Singhji.

Juhi Chawla: It was at this holy spot that Guruji commanded that the tradition being followed all this while—of worshipping a human guru—be discontinued and henceforth all devotion and worship be vested in the Guru Granth Sahib. 'Do not bow before anybody, if you have to show respect or bow, do so before the Guru Granth Sahib,' he said. He established the Guru Granth Sahib with such honour that it was inclusive of not only Sikh gurus but also Hindus, Muslims and those of the Harijan sect.

Devotee 22: All the religions are assimilated in the Guru Granth Sahib. Along with that of the Gurus, there are also sayings of Kabir and Ravi Das. The message is that it is not just a holy book of the Sikh faith but of all four religions. These sayings are the true inheritance of all the Sikh Gurus.

Devotee 23: Actually, it is the eternal, ever-living Guru for us.

Devotee 24: Sleep and whatever else we get is all because of this Guru.

Devotee 25: When we read or listen to it being said, our hearts are filled with contentment.

Juhi Chawla: It is not in our power to gauge the greatness of the Guru. It is illimitable and subject to devotion. It is said that the lentils served in the blessed food to devotees can even cure mental illness.

Devotee 26: This is the blessed food offered to Guru Maharaj. This has been continuing for centuries.

Devotee 27: When Guru Gobind Singhji had come here, when his end was near, the Pathans had struck him. They had struck him on the stomach with a sharp dagger. Then, with arrows, his wound was made even more grievous. The Sikhs then planned to bring him a doctor (hakim). When the hakim arrived, he suggested that a special lentil soup be given to him to drink—this would allow his internal injuries to dry up and heal.

Devotee 28: Ever since then, the tradition of drinking lentil soup for curing illnesses has continued.

Devotee 29: Whoever has this will have their sorrows, pain and problems taken away.

Devotee 30: Someone from another caste had come from Delhi—he could not walk. After the worshipping ceremonies were over, he just had to come here and have the lentil soup every day. We had been observing for three–four months that he had been walking in a strange manner. After that he began walking absolutely straight.

Devotee 31: This is not just for curing illnesses, but for feeling comforted as well.

Devotee 32: It is just Guruji that we depend on. Whatever is asked of him, we get. We come and sit at his feet. I am more than eighty years old and I can happily say he has given me everything.

Juhi Chawla: The word 'Sikh' has evolved from the Sanskrit word 'Sishya', meaning student. All beings born on this earth, while traversing the path to moksha, have to learn to focus and take the name of God. A good student becomes one who understands what he has learnt from this education. 'Seva', or service, is a very important part of the Sikh religion. Wherever there is need of any help or service, the sevadar is present. That is why whenever there is any need, all members of the Sikh community come together in service.

Devotee 33: The two friends of Sikhism are simran (remembrance) and seva. Simran means to remember the Almighty all the time. Seva believes that if the body that has been given to us can be put to use and be of assistance to someone, it should be.

Devotee 34: We, the sevaks, serve without any greed or desire for personal gain. We try to offer something to the Guru of our own volition.

Devotee 35 (a foreigner): The whole point of Sikhism is to beat the ego—because that is what makes you think, 'I am this, I am that...' And when you do sangat—which means service to all and sharing work at the gurudwara—it is to lessen the ego. And when you can do that, Wahe Guru enters you. That is why people serve, and they do it voluntarily.

Devotee 36: There is peace in service. There is joy, and it feels like being part of one family while working here.

Devotee 37: Service is everything—one learns to bow low and there is a feeling of reverence.

Devotee 38: So many people come here from such great distances; we get an opportunity to touch the ground they have walked on. Who knows which great seer has come in what guise? If we touch the feet of some such person, our lives will be fulfilled.

Devotee 39: There is a feeling of great joy when any kind of service is rendered—whether it is washing utensils or general cleanliness or tending to the shoes. There is nothing like too high up or too low down for us, and differences of age do not matter.

Juhi Chawla: Langar is a prime example of togetherness and brotherhood. In this meal, there is no difference between the rich and the poor—there is no distinction. The most remarkable factor is everyone takes their seat on the ground and has their meal. This continues round the clock. If anyone turns up, we are always there. Food is always ready to be served. If the food gets over, cooking starts again in ten minutes; even as you take his name, the food is ready.

Devotee 40: It is Guru Gobind Singh who is doing everything.

Devotee 41: The only prayer that I have is, 'Please give me a chance to serve here. There is nothing more to ask for, there is nothing that I want.'

Devotee 42: There is an out-of-the-world feeling here, because you are leaving behind business, work and everything else. There is no tension. You are coming here, staying with the Guru, serving and praying (Shukrani Ardas). It is simple. The mind is refreshed and gears up for the next year. One year just seems to fly by and we know that we have to return.

Juhi Chawla: In Hazur Sahib, all the teachings, lessons and rituals taught by the gurus down the ages are still followed with fervour and devotion. Of this one is Gagar ki Rasam. Early in the morning, carrying empty pitchers, devotees walk about a mile to the Godavari River and, amid the chanting of the Holy One's name, return with filled pitchers. This water is used to wash and cleanse the room and doorway of the Guru every day.

On coming here it seems that one has become immersed in the melodious rhythm of kirtans.

After the auspicious reading of the Rehras (commonly known as Rehras Sahib or Sodar Rehras, it is the daily evening prayer of the Sikhs and is part of Nitnem), the aarti and kirtans take place.

Devotee 43: The Guruvani is heard all around, which fills the heart will serenity. His memories seem to permeate every corner.

Devotee 44: You feel a connect with God here. When you see something holy in front of you, you truly feel that God is not far away, but all around you.

Juhi Chawla: The place where the Sikh Community gathers and listens to the words of advice and holy songs of their gurus is known as a gurudwara, or gateway to the guru. This is the ultimate doorway.

Devotee 45: When one submits to the Guru, he himself takes charge of everything and fulfils all wants and desires. I have this belief in the Guru.

Devotee 46: When I come here, there is a lot that I want, but when I am here, there is nothing I can ask for. When I am in this place, all that I could have asked for has already been fulfilled because I have seen You, O God.

Devotee 47: The one who gives us all is here. Look at the Almighty in any form, He is everywhere.

Devotee 48: The Lord hears the sound of even an ant. So if we call from the heart, the Almighty will listen.

Devotee 49: Everybody has their own beliefs. I have this conviction that I have to go to the gurudwara—I will go, and go again.

16

MAHAKALESHWAR TEMPLE

The city of temples, Ujjain, in Madhya Pradesh, is steeped in faith and devotion. Each fragment of Ujjain, with its powerful mysticism, speaks of Lord Shankar in its own unique way. No matter where you are within the city, you seem to be magically pulled towards the enigmatic temple of Mahakaleshwar. Lord Shiva is believed to have self-manifested in the form of lingams, called Jyotirlingas, at twelve locations around the country, of which the temple of Mahakaleshwar is one. It is the focal point of the city, and Mahakal, as Lord Shiva is known here, is not only the guardian and patron deity, but is also regarded as the ruler of this city, mightier than time itself.

Juhi Chawla: When there was nothing, He was omnipresent. When there will be utter emptiness, He will still be there. For aeons, people have an ingrained belief that there is a mystical power that has tied together so many millions of people. Sometimes with hands raised in faith and sometimes with hands folded in obeisance; sometimes carrying thalis of holy offerings, and at others bearing the holy books in faith—through these, all of us are engaged in a continual search for Him.

I, Juhi Chawla, will take you on such a sojourn, which is a unification of all such feelings, which traverses thousands of miles and draws people to the places where we may find Him. The experience of that faith, this journey, is of the conviction that we will.

With desire and hope in the heart, your devotee has come to you. You are the Father and the Mother too. Your protective shadow lies over us. The darkness that submits to any light, that illumination, Mahadev (Shiva), is nothing but your shadow.

Devotee 1: There is always a lot of tension in my mind, a lot of thoughts—but whenever I catch a glimpse of Him, it feels that someone has laid a hand of assurance on my head and that matters will get sorted out. It feels like there is nothing in life but joy. I then return with that positivity.

Devotee 2: I have had a bypass surgery and am over sixty-five years of age; yet there is no sense of tiredness at all when I am here.

Devotee 3: It feels very good here and there is a lot of peace. It feels like we have come to a place like heaven.

Devotee 4: This place gives us the strength to bear every sorrow. If there is a problem, we leave it to Him, and it does not feel like there is any issue at all.

Devotee 5: There has never been any problem Baba has not shown me a solution to. He has given me the answer every time. In life when I had no solutions I had come to Him.

Devotee 6: There is something in the soil here, a magnetic pull, such that even if you think you won't go that day, something will draw you there.

Devotee 7: What I really want is to construct a house here, and pray to Him morning and evening.

Juhi Chawla: Ujjain is the pilgrim centre of all pilgrim centres, where each pebble seems to assume the form of Lord Shiva. This is why no matter which alley you take, all paths will lead you to the Mahakaleshwar Temple. Situated on the eastern coast of the Shipra River, this ancient city is taken to be the focal point of all religious activity.

Devotee 8: This is an ancient city, which was named Avantika prior to Ujjain.

Devotee 9: This is a limitless city, with no boundaries. It has been here since the very beginning—it was there when even the universe wasn't formed and will continue to remain when the world will cease to be.

Devotee 10: All gods and goddesses have come here— Ram, Lakshman and Janaki, too, stepped on this soil; Lord Krishna's place of education was also here for a while.

Devotee 11: I had been hearing a lot about this place for a very long time. So I wondered what was so special about it. Why were people so attracted to it? So I came here to see for myself, and now I understand.

Devotee 12: When I started off, I had virtually nothing, not even slippers. But I had faith in Mahakal, and He gave me everything.

Devotee 13: Mahakaleshwar Bhagwan is everything to me and after that comes my father, mother and the entire family.

Devotee couple: Never had we thought that a day would come when we would actually be able to visit and pay our respects to Mahakaleshwar. Today is a day in life when the Lord has called us. All praise be with Him.

Juhi Chawla: The tall temple seems to converse with the skies, and it appears that Lord Shiva has decided to reside here. The head bows in respect to Him.

Devotee 14: It seems to be my good fortune that I have come here and been able to see Him. My life seems worthwhile.

Devotee 15: All the mental tension and worries vanish when we take shelter under Him.

Devotee 16: Without paying respects to Him, my day does not go well. It has been fifteen years since I started coming here.

Devotee 17: Once we get here, we do not feel like going back. Inexpressible peace seems to surround us.

Juhi Chawla: This is that spot where Lord Shiva embodied the eternal truth in the form of a Jyotirlinga. This form, created by the Lord Himself, seems to be Shiva's own home, where all of nature seems to assemble.

Ashish Sharma (temple priest): Just as the midpoint of

our body is the navel, similarly among the chakras it is the Manipur Chakra. It is on that Manipur Chakra that Mahakaal is evident.

Juhi Chawla: One who far surpasses even time, one who Himself gives birth to death, he Himself is Mahakal—our respectful obeisance to Him.

Devotee 18: This is where 'kal', or time, begins. He is the overlord of time. Hence He is worshipped here.

Devotee 19: Mrityunjoy is Mahakal. If one comes here and utters the Mrityunjoy incantation, all fear and problems are done away with.

Devotee 20: I was very scared of death and so someone suggested that I come here.

Juhi Chawla: One who is greater than time itself, Mahakal, finds his place in the temple here. There are a lot of stories about how His name came to be 'Mahakal'.

There is a tale that a Brahmin and his four sons were engaged in prayer. The Brahmin who was conducting the prayers asked his spiritual mentor what this place was where he was praying. The answer was that since all eternity Mahakal resides there.

In the Ratnamala mountains lived a demon named Dushan. Brahma had granted him the boon of being unconquerable. When he got to know about a family who were devotees of Shiva and the Vedas, armed with a great number of demon soldiers he attacked the city, Avanti. Despite this fearsome attack, however, the Brahmin and his family retained their faith in Shiva and, unafraid, continued meditating. Just as the demon was about to strike them, there was a thunderous noise. The phallic stone disappeared and in its place appeared a deep gorge from which rose a fearsome avatar of Shiva. The flames emitting from Him destroyed the world. By His mere breath Shiva destroyed Dushan and all the other demons. The Brahmins folded their hands and prayed that for the betterment of mankind Lord Shiva be transformed again.

Ashish Sharma: Shiva agreed and said that from that day He would remain at that spot and be worshipped as Mahakal.

Juhi Chawla: In this destructible earthly realm, the Shiva linga established at the Mahakaleshwar temple has special powers. This is felt by every single devotee who comes here.

Devotee 21: That sense of happiness will never be felt by anyone else. You will get goosebumps when you catch sight of Baba, and if you touch Him, you will feel that you have attained everything in life.

Devotee 22: I felt that my Bholenath was with me and was blessing me. His limitless kindness is showered on me.

Devotee 23: At that time it seems that nothing and no one exists but Him and me. We are one.

Devotee 24: I lose myself after going there. There is a continual conversation between Lord Shiva and me. These feelings cannot be described or put into words.

Devotee 25: When we emerge from the temple, it seems that we are one. Inside, it seems that we are in heaven.

Devotee 26: This is like an atomic power plant. It seems that even if I imbibe .01 per cent of the power here and feel it within me, I will be blessed.

Ascetic: There is a great feeling of romance here. It feels as though strains from a hundred tunes are playing in my heart; thousands of lotuses seem to be blooming. I feel supreme joy when I touch the linga or the phallic stone.

Devotee 27: I have done this thrice. The first time I went, I did not know and took away the flowers. Then I found out that aarti was being carried out and I re-entered. Then after participating in the aarti, people were pushing me outside. But it seems fate directed me to go to the rear of the temple and pour water on the linga. I bowed low and genuflected before him.

Devotee 28: I had come last night, too, to pay my respects. It was with great difficulty that I had five minutes, but then I was told that I could only try to see Him—if Mahakal wanted me to see Him I would. The gates had closed, but I was still able to catch a glimpse of Him. What more could I want?

Juhi Chawla: The most chaste seat of Bholenath is our mind. That has been His place since eternity, and His loving glance, full of empathy, is showered on us. People of all caste, creed and community come here and receive the blessings of Mahadev.

Devotee 29: I have been praying to Shivji ever since I was a child. Coming here, it feels like I have to keep coming back; I try to come at least once a year.

Devotee 30: I had chikungunya. I have come here with the hope that the ache in the hands and the feet goes away.

Devotee 31: Last year, I had come here with a few dreams with my partner—and this year we have got married. So I have come to pay my respects to Him.

Devotee 32: Whenever I come here, I think there are certain things that I will ask for, for myself and members of my family. But when I do come here, I find that I cannot say a word—He knows everything. What I want or do not want—everything is obtained.

Devotee couple: Whatever I want, He gives me. Whatever I think of, He gives me. He fulfils all my desires.

Juhi Chawla: The people of Ujjain have an unbreakable bond with Mahakal. That is why no matter what the daily chores, the ancient Hindu rituals have a bond that cannot be broken. No sooner does one enter the city than there is a magnetic pull that draws one to the temple.

Devotee 33: As soon as we even start the journey from home, of eleven hours, it seems that we have already seen God.

Devotee 34: All my problems, pain and tiredness vanish when I enter the temple premises. There is nothing else and I can only see Mahakal. There is just a desire to see Him and once that is done, there is satisfaction.

Devotee 35: It feels as though Bholenath has called out to us to come to Him.

Devotee 36: It seems that I am called every day, and I pray that I am always called in such a manner.

Priest: Our primary task is to allow people to have their fill of looking at Mahakal.

Devotee 37: I look at Baba and say that I have to return again.

Juhi Chawla: The bodies and minds of the devotees here are replete with devotion. It seems like the love of both mother and father has been showered on them.

Devotee 38: His presence is everywhere—whether in the front or at the rear.

Devotee 39: No sooner do I take His name than I feel energized and, of course, I have also witnessed the influence that He has.

Devotee 40: I was hit by four bullets, and my liver, along with other internal organs, was damaged. It was pretty critical. The doctors had said that I would not survive—but it is because of His kindness that I am standing here today.

Preeti Chauhan (admin officer, Mahakal temple): I was a housewife, and then I lost my husband and child. I felt that it could only be Baba Mahakal who could cradle me in His arms and carry me through this—otherwise I would have broken down.

Devotee 41: I was in print media in Mumbai, and in the fast life I led, I forgot my limitations—from where I have come and where I have reached in society. I went back to my native place and started learning the alphabets again. When I returned and started a new life, it was from here itself.

Devotee 42: This is His mystical munificence. If you remember Him with reverence, think of Him with reverence, miracles will happen.

Juhi Chawla: The kindness of Mahadev in the form of Mahakal has been showered on this world for eternity. It is believed that if one catches even a glimpse of Him, the doors to eternal bliss are thrown open.

Devotee 43: My heart is at peace; it is my good fortune that I have been able to reach this point. Now all that I pray for is that the Lord help me in crossing over to the other side. I have everything in life.

Devotee 44: We go to the house of the Almighty to extend our thanks and gratitude to Him, but inevitably we end up asking for more. All those who go there to have their wishes fulfilled ultimately end up asking for moksha.

Juhi Chawla: Every single hour remains immersed in the love of the Lord and it is impossible to describe in words the beauty of the early-morning hours. The only reverberation is that of Bholenath's name; all devotees make their way to participate in the Jal Abhishek, or water worship.

Devotee 45: The doors are opened at 4.00 in the morning. Then there are various rituals that take place one after the other.

Juhi Chawla: At the end of the ritualistic bathing, He is adorned; from being without any form, there is a form that is given to Him. He turns into Shankar.

Then the special 'bhasma aarti' takes place. In the particulars mentioned in our scriptures, Shiva is worshipped with certain incantations and ashes are used. After this Lord Shiva is worshipped. When the lights are turned off, it seems that Baba is standing right in front, and it feels as though a wave of electricity is running through the body. When these morning rituals are carried out, there is nothing comparable to the ambience that is created.

The temple of Mahakal welcomes everyone. He is the mentor and also the one who showers pity. He is the father of all. The easiest way to be at one with Him is to be like a child, showering love and devotion without any complication.

17

KRISHNA BALARAM TEMPLE

A place nestled on the holy banks of the Yamuna, resonating with the amusing tricks of young Krishna and echoing with the gaiety of the gopis, Vrindavan can rightfully be termed the playground of the beloved Lord Krishna. Almost every nook and corner of this holy city speaks to you about the playful escapades of the compassionate cowherd brothers, Krishna and Balaram. Once you enter Vrindavan, the radiance and stillness in the air is unmistakable. Walking along the bustling thoroughfare of the city, you reach the beatific Krishna Balaram Temple. Enveloped in a blissful ambience of devotion and holiness, the temple of ISKCON (International Society for Krishna Consciousness) has a sacred appeal that pulls everyone towards it with an undeniable charm. It is believed that the two brothers, Krishna and Balaram, used to play and amuse the residents of Vrindavan with their antics here. A visit to the Krishna Balaram Temple leaves your soul stirred with divine love and peace.

Juhi Chawla: When there was nothing, He was omnipresent. When there will be utter emptiness, He will still be there. For aeons, people have an ingrained belief that there is a mystical power that has tied together so many millions of people. Sometimes with hands raised in faith and sometimes with hands folded in obeisance; sometimes carrying thalis of holy offerings, and at others bearing the holy books in faith—through these, all of us are engaged in a continual search for Him.

I, Juhi Chawla, will take you on such a sojourn, which is a unification of all such feelings, which traverses thousands of miles and draws people to the places where we may find Him. The experience of that faith, this journey, is of the conviction that we will.

Devotee 1: The more you take the name of the Lord, the more you will bear His name in your heart; He is the one who will help you cross all barriers. *Jai Sri Radhe Shyam*!

Devotee 2: When there's harsh sunlight and the wind blows, the soothing cool breeze is only felt under a tree. I stay in Agra, but the cool and soothing balmy wind is only felt here.

Devotee 3: Whenever you come to pay your respects to Him, be it once a year or five times a day, there is a satisfaction that I have now reached the right place. There is a desire that now that we have reached Him, let our soul also leave the body here.

Devotee 4: 'Ram Naam Satya Hain' is generally recited at the time of death—what is the use of people reciting this when you are gone? It should be said every day. There will be joy and all sorrow will vanish.

Juhi Chawla: About 160 km from Delhi is situated Vrindavan Dham. There in every nook and corner flows the love of Krishna Consciousness.

Devotee 5 (a local): Kashi is believed to be the place for attaining freedom. In a similar manner, Vrindavan Dham is believed to be the place of devotion and love. Here you will see the greatest love and devotion.

Devotee 6: Here, the atmosphere is divine, the waters of the Yamuna are divine, the very air has touched the Almighty and is also divine. There is the presence of God everywhere.

Juhi Chawla: In Vrindavan, there's a strong bond of love between God and man.

Devotee 7: With the lilting sweetness of Kanha's flute, every wave of the Yamuna becomes a melody. God is everywhere, but Vrindavan is the veritable image of Krishna. There is nothing more than that. 'Vrindavan' means the house of the Lord.

Devotee 8: This locale is not regarded as being on earth but in heaven. It is the expansion of God's house here. So here nobody can remain unhappy.

Devotee 9 (elderly lady): I am very happy here and the day I am unable to come, I know I will weep.

Devotee 10: When my son got into college, I thought of going to Vrindavan and staying there for six months; and the other six months I thought I would return to America. I had come with an open ticket of three months, but Radha Rani is so kind that she did not permit me to leave. It has been eleven years that I have been here in Vrindavan and have never gone back, and neither will I. Vrindavan is a place of joy.

Devotee 11: As soon as I wake up every day, I pray that I am allowed to stay in Vrindavan all my life.

Juhi Chawla: This place is known as the city of love, the Brijkshetra, redolent with fragrance and beautifully decorated. The sensations that are felt here are similar to actually feeling the presence of Lord Krishna here. No sooner do devotees reach Vrindavan than all their problems vanish. The poverty- and malady-stricken are taken care of and protected.

Devotee 12: It feels He is beside me and always with me. Whenever there is any moment of sorrow, or any problem, it feels like He is right here. Just feeling that drives my problems away.

Devotee 13 (young man): If you take the name of Krishna, be it anywhere, all your problems and sorrows are bound to disappear. All that is needed is to take His name.

Devotee 14: The only thing He is thinking is how to make the residents of Brijdham (Vrindavan) happy—or Brajajana-ranjana (Braja is Vrindavan, 'jana' means people and 'ranjana' means happy). How can he make the gopis happy? How can he make the cows happy? That is all Krishna thinks about.

Devotee 15: When we take a step towards Krishna, He takes ten steps towards us. He is merciful. It is not that this is imaginary—God is present there.

Juhi Chawla: Sri Krishna is the child of Vrindavan. It has witnessed Him frolic with the gopis. He had even lifted the entire Govardhan Parvat on His little finger to shelter His devotees from rain.

Devotee 16: When Indradev had made it rain continuously for seven days, Sri Krishna had lifted Govardhan Mountain on the tip of his little finger. After the rains had stopped, He put Govardhan back, and there was a huge festival.

Juhi Chawla: Govardhan Parvat is a symbol of empathy, of the unending love that Krishna feels for His devotees. In respect of that love and devotion, all devotees make their way to His temple to pay respects to Him.

Devotee 17: Since February 1994 I have been doing this and continue to every month.

Devotee 18: I started coming here when I was about fifteen years old, and now I am almost fifty.

Devotee 19: This is my third time; I have covered 21 km, but there is no hunger or thirst in me.

Devotee 20: My name is Madan Mohan Walia and I am from Delhi. I have been coming here for the past ten years. There is no ulterior motive or any demand in my mind. This is purely out of devotion—in the hope that I will actually meet God some day.

Devotee 21: I have tried coming here thrice, but each time I was unable to. I come regularly, but only when it is His will am I able to do so.

Devotee 22: I have been travelling to various places ever since I was a child. Anybody who undertakes this sojourn will definitely come in close proximity to Him.

Devotee 23: I like it so much here that I am even fond of whatever weather this places throws up—whether sunny or raining or just cold. Even walking appeals to me. I get blisters sometimes, but it does not really matter.

Devotee 24: What I am doing or what I am searching for or what I am seeing does not matter. All that matters is that Sri Krishna is here.

Juhi Chawla: This parikrama is all about dedication to the love felt for Sri Krishna. This great journey is a journey of faith and the feeling of joy.

Devotee 25: We belong to Him and our emotions also belong to Him. This is something you feel.

Devotee 26: In 1988 I had a severe accident and there was a crack in my bones. If my fracture were to be X-rayed today, the doctor would surely ask if I was brought in on a wheelchair or a stretcher. On my last visit to the doctor, I was asked how much I walk. And I replied that I walk 21 km of circumambulation.

Foreign devotee: Vrindavan is a very special place and every step you take is a parikrama. Here, even sleeping is Dandavat (prostrating oneself in front of the Lord).

Juhi Chawla: I have not seen Lord Krishna, but I have heard Him around me. In the alleys of Vrindavan, I have heard the tinkling sound of the anklets of Radha. When the name of Krishna has been taken with true devotion, there has been the fragrance of butter all around. Without even realizing it, we find ourselves moving towards the holy place where Balaram and Krishna lived.

At a distance of 2 km from Vrindavan, one finds the Krishna-Balaram Mandir, also known as the ISKCON Temple. Devotees come here to imbibe the spirit of Krishna.

Devotee 27: Since I have seen Shayamsunder, read him, felt him, I feel He is my own parents, my family. They all are close to me.

Devotee 28: The temple is my home. The entire day I am in the temple, and I cannot imagine life without it.

Devotee 29: Everyone who comes here has different sensations. Nobody can actually express how they feel. Anyone you ask will give you the same answer—that if you come here, you won't want to leave.

Juhi Chawla:

> The beautiful two eyes of Brijbumi
> Without seeing whom there is no peace
> In whom dwells the life of devotees
> One is Krishna and the other Balaram

In Vrindavan images of Radha and Krishna are seen everywhere. What is special about this temple and what attracts me greatly is that both brothers, Krishna and Balaram, are together and it is a magnificently attractive picture.

Elderly couple: There are three altars here. In the central altar is Krishna-Balaram, on the right are Radha-Shyamsunder, and on the left is Gour Nitai.

Devotee 30: When we are close to the altar it feels that my batteries are being recharged. It feels that I have been imbued with new life, my lifeless body has been brought back to life.

Devotee 31: We are transported to another world altogether—whether Gokul or Baikunth—when we catch a glimpse of Krishna-Balaram.

Devotee 32: It so happens that there is a different kind of feeling in this temple. Krishna-Balaram, Radhe-Shyam—there is a feeling that whenever there is some kind of problem, I can go straight to God.

Juhi Chawla: This is that magical spot of Vrindavan, the ISKCON Temple, where devotees cast aside their worries, and dance with their hands raised in joy. ISKCON is the first of the international temples that was constructed in 1975 by Swami Prabhupadji. We spoke with Dharmatmaji, who is the secretary of the temple.

Dharmatma Das (secretary): The ISKCON is how to have our thoughts enveloped in Krishna Consciousness.

Devotee 33: Prabhupad came here in 1970 and said that he wanted to have a temple constructed here.

Dharmatma Das: Prabhupad named this temple Krishna-Balaram Mandir. You will have seen that the image of the two of them is at the centre because the name of this place is Raman Reti.

Devotee 34: This is the place where Krishna and Balaram used to play with their friends and with the cows. They used to go to the Yamuna. That is why, watching all this,

Sri Prabhupad made this Raman Reti in front of this temple.

Juhi Chawla: The Raman Reti Dham of Gokul has been blessed by the divine footfall of Krishna and Balaram. Even now when the devotees touch the earth there, they are infused with joy. According to the Vedas and the Puranas, whenever some great danger is to befall the earth, Lord Vishnu in some form or the other will appear to save mankind, with His favourite Sheshnag. Sheshnag appeared as Lakshman in the Treta Yug and as Balaram in the Dwapar Yug; Lord Krishna always used to address them as Dao, or bhaiya.

Devotee 35: There is a saying in Braj that the king of Braj is Dada Dau! Here he is not known as Balaram, but Dau Dada. 'Dada' means elder brother.

Devotee 36: Balaram and Krishna are the same; Balaramji is just an extension of Krishna.

Devotee 37: In any worship, Balaram is taken to be the virtual embodiment of all musical instruments. He is known as the Adya Guru because all the information we have today has been in the image of Balaramji.

Devotee 38: Krishna and Balaram are the same.

Devotee 39: Krishna is one who attracts everybody.

Juhi Chawla: Krishna is a stream of contentment and joy. Anyone who is inspired by the knowledge of knowing Him becomes devoted to Him, always moving along the path of self-realization.

Dharmatma Das: When we keep God at the centre of our being, our lives are bound to be calm, peaceful and serene.

Juhi Chawla: The Krishna-Balaram Mandir is a symbol of the love and respect devotees feel for the god they worship. Here, devotees remain immersed in thoughts of Kanhaiya, or Krishna. Devotees of all ages dance and chant 'Hare Rama Hare Krishna'.

Devotee 40: If you say 'Hare Krishna' even once, you will feel like doing so again.

Devotee 41: It is stated in the Gita that Sri Krishna, Radha Rani and Balaram dance on the tip of our tongues.

Devotee 42: It is just like the call of a child to his parents.

Devotee 43 (a local): This chanting and incantation goes on for twenty-four hours. Anyone who goes feels great joy. Nobody feels like leaving.

Juhi Chawla: In loud tones devotees take the name of the Lord Krishna when they worship him. They bow their heads and seek His blessings. Devotees forget the world in their love for Krishna. Some become Meera and others Radha.

Dharmatma Das: When we dance and raise our hands, people of the seven lokas above are happy; when our feet touch the ground, the people of this world are sanctified.

Juhi Chawla: Millions of voices, all calling out the name of Krishna, hands folded in love and prayer, want just this through their dance—allow us to see You and be with us in each birth. If we cannot find You, You come to us.

18

NAKODA BHAIRAV TEMPLE

Some throng this temple to ask for blessings and fill themselves with hope and peace. Others come here to thank the deity every day for fulfilling their wishes. No matter the reason, everyone who walks into the Nakoda Bhairav Temple in Rajasthan leaves with a heart full of devotion, hope and joy.

Juhi Chawla: When there was nothing, He was omnipresent. When there will be utter emptiness, He will still be there. For aeons, people have an ingrained belief that there is a mystical power that has tied together so many millions of people. Sometimes with hands raised in faith and sometimes with hands folded in obeisance; sometimes carrying thalis of holy offerings, and at others bearing the holy books in faith—through these, all of us are engaged in a continual search for Him.

I, Juhi Chawla, will take you on such a sojourn, which is a unification of all such feelings, which traverses thousands of miles and draws people to the places where we may find Him. The experience of that faith, this journey, is of the conviction that we will.

Devotee 1: The sense of devotion that permeates here is very peaceful.

Devotee 2: You come here for yourself and see—it will seem that you are sitting in front of God yourself.

Devotee 3 (old man): One enters with reverence, and with reverence everything can be achieved. The heart wants to catch a glimpse of the Almighty.

Devotee 4: It feels good to me and I love this. It's like I am a child. I cannot stay without going to the temple even one day. I have a lot of reverence for the God.

Devotee 5: The atmosphere here is so positive, all negativity goes away.

Devotee 6: When we are in the presence of the Almighty, the head automatically bows low. Anyone who comes here does so with a feeling that something good will come of it.

Juhi Chawla: Who says that anyone who comes here is poverty-stricken? The person who reaches You is the most fortunate. About 125 km from the city of Jodhpur in Rajasthan, situated among the sentinel mountains, in Nakoda—the internationally renowned pilgrim centre of the Jains—is the Nakoda Paraswanath Temple.

Ashok Chopra (temple trustee): This temple dates back to the third century, but construction was completed in 1502. This is a very important place for us Jains.

Devotee 7: Jains and non-Jains are all welcome here.

Devotee 8: We have been coming here for the past fifty years at least.

Devotee 9 (young girl): I am Jyoti Palkia from Kolkata. This is probably the fourth or the fifth time I am coming here.

Devotee 10: There is a lot of peace when one comes here. There is a different kind of sensation, which perhaps cannot be expressed in words.

Devotee 11: When we come here we feel fully charged.

Devotee 12 (young couple): No matter who comes here, their hopes and prayers are always granted.

Devotee 13: I had suffered from a heart attack. I prayed to Bhairoji and I was saved.

Devotee 14: I did not have a child and God gave me one after ten years. What more can I ask for?

Juhi Chawla: This is a place where it is said that even danger is scared to tread. Devotion is nurtured in the lap of belief. Thousands of devotees from all over the world seek shelter in the God they worship. He is the twenty-third tirthankara, Guru Paraswanath.

Devotee 15: Bhagwan Paraswanath has 108 forms and names. Some are renowned, such as Nakoda; others are Jeerawala, Nageswar, and so on.

Devotee 16: Go anywhere in India, you will see that Bhagwan Paraswanath's pilgrimage centres outnumber any other god's. This era belongs to Mahavir Bhagwan but Paraswanath has outnumbered him, too, in terms of temples and pilgrimage centres.

Devotee 17: I am a Rajput but the Jain religion is so chaste that I appreciate the norms and regulations it follows. Paraswanathji has such unbreakable rules that there is no need to say that it emanates from the soul.

Juhi Chawla: The Jains accept the tirthankaras as their gods. Those who can conquer lust, hatred, desire, depression and sorrow, and can free the inner soul from the circle of rebirth, that tirthankar is also known as Jina (victor). The blessings of the protective Nakoda Bhairav are a magnetic draw. He is regarded as the protector of the city and of the religion. Whatever is wished for from the protector is granted. All wishes of devotees are fulfilled.

Devotee 18: In 1987 I was in a great deal of trouble, and I prayed—within half an hour the matter was resolved.

Devotee 19: I fell down and had a haemorrhage. At that time, Bhairav Dada's name had emerged from my mouth. That is why I am still standing today.

Juhi Chawla: He, the Lord of the Life Cycle, Bhairodev is in full support of his devotees. Only if the tirthankar, too, is alongside, can all troubles and problems be done away with. The strength of belief is so great that even birth and death can be conquered.

Devotee 20: In the Jain religion, the role of Nakoda Paraswanath Bhagwan is very important. Bhairavji also plays a vital role.

Devotee 21: Whenever we come here, sorrows, problems and difficulties vanish.

Juhi Chawla: When devotees enter the temple premises, the romance and mysticism in the ambience comes alive. When the devotees see the powerful image of Bhairav, there is so much joy in the heart that it feels like your feet are not touching the ground any more.

Devotee 22: It feels so good that Dada is so merciful to us and keeps such a vigilant eye on us.

Devotee 23: Even if you focus a little and gaze at his eyes, they will speak to you.

Devotee 24: O Lord, please be part of me while I am alive; when my eyes finally close, be part of me then too.

Juhi Chawla: Bhairav, the one who finds a place in a thousand minds on the threshold of their dreams, that very God is immersed in the greatness of Paraswanath Bhagwan. The voice of Nakoda Bhairav is focused on Paraswaprabhu.

Devotee 25: Even one thousand years ago, there was a Jain temple here. Now the image there is of Nakoda Paraswanath Bhagwan.

Devotee 26: A man had a dream and it is because of that that he tried to take out from the reservoir an image which was named Nakoda Paraswanath. But despite all efforts the image just could not be taken out. The people were puzzled and did not know what to do. So they decided to go to a holy man. They went to Acharya Kirtiratan Surji Maharaj. The acharya prayed to the local deity, who was very helpful and said that the image should be lifted on the head.

Juhi Chawla: Acharya Kirtiratan Surji Maharaj picked up the image of Paraswanath and went to establish the image, with the crowds growing behind him. In that procession, Nakoda Bhairav, in the guise of a child, was seen dancing in joy and leading the way.

Devotee 27 (a local): Paraswanath Bhagwan moved from there to here. That is how Nakoda Paraswanath Bhagwan Parmatma became added to it.

Juhi Chawla: That day onwards, if anyone approaches with hope in their hearts, Nakoda Bhairav never disheartens them. The lamp of hope glows a million times brighter because of the blessings of Paraswanath. The true path—of religion, knowledge and Jina—is shown to millions of devotees even today.

Devotee 28: If anybody has any problems at home or medical issues, if they pray to Him wholeheartedly, the issue is bound to be resolved.

Devotee 29: We were in dire straits financially. My father has always been a devotee and I also started coming here. Since then, we have never looked back. Every time we were just taking a step forward.

Devotee 30 (elderly couple): Just eight or ten days ago my son got married. It seemed to me that Bhairu Dada was there: every time the programme began, the rains would stop, and resume when the programme was over. There were no problems at all.

Devotee 31 (young woman): Nakoda Bhairav is Dev and Kshatrapal Baba, or the protector of the directions. Even in this era of Kalyug, he places his hand of protection on us.

Juhi Chawla: Nakoda has been named the Tirupathi of Northwest India. People come here from all over the world. It does not matter if the devotee comes empty-handed, his heart should be full of faith. A pure heart full of devotion is very dear to God.

Devotee 32: You can offer fruits or dry fruits. Gowli is something that we make from rice and mark with the swastika and certain other symbols. Even spices, herbs and dry fruits are offered.

Juhi Chawla: These offerings are part of what the local businessmen and the business community at large offer Nakoda Bhairav of their own volition.

Devotee 33: Devotees offer whatever they can afford, depending on their livelihood and income.

Devotee 34: Whatever is left at the end of the financial year and whatever they can manage, they put in.

Juhi Chawla: There is a unique tradition followed before the first worship of the day begins at Bhairodev. There is a kind of auction among the devotees to decide who will be responsible for the first puja ceremony of the day.

Devotee 35: According to the Jain religion, everyone is given the opportunity to serve the temple and offer that day's puja. It is not that it only goes to the person doing the puja. That is why there is an auction first and then everyone does it in turn.

Devotee 36: Sometimes at the fair and festivities of Paush Dashami, the auctions can go up to lakhs of kilogrammes.

Juhi Chawla: For those who are unable to do so, it is not that Bhairav moves away from them; rather He draws closer.

Devotee 37: Joss sticks are lit and other rituals are carried out; then the reflection of the Lord's image is seen in the mirror. A prayer is then sent up to the Lord. The reflection in the mirrors is like the Lord's reflection in our bodies. It is to help us remain pure and chaste.

Devotee 38: We look at His image in the mirror and say, 'When will we become like You?'

Devotee 39: The only intention is to invite the Lord into our hearts, so that everything in life becomes pure and chaste. We pray we do not have to be born again and again. There is no death for one who is not born.

Juhi Chawla: When on the threshold of devotion the lamps of faith are lit, even pitch darkness is dispelled. Wrapped in this cloak of faith, thousands of devotees worship Prabhu Paraswanath and Nakoda Bhairav through the mornings and the evenings. First, the aarti is dedicated to Paraswanath and then to Nakoda Bhairav. The sweetness of the devotion, along with the tinkling of bells, infuses everyone with so much piety that the image of Nakoda almost comes to life and finds a home in the hearts of the devotees. Each breath drawn is heavy with the essence of faith.

Devotee 40: If you are devotedly thinking of God and praying to Him, not only will you see Him, but your wishes will also be fulfilled.

Devotee 41: The one who prays most devotedly to Bhairavji is assimilated in Him and is even given a glimpse of Him in the evening.

Devotee 42: We are happy when we come but sad when we leave, thinking about when the Lord will call us again.

19

KAAL BHAIRAV TEMPLE

Varanasi, also known as Kashi or Benares, is one of the oldest cities in India. Soaked in divinity and dipped in holiness, Varanasi is considered a melting pot, a place where both life and death merge seamlessly. Hindus across the world believe in staying at Kashi during their final days to greet death and attain moksha. It is widely accepted among Hindus that permission to stay at Varanasi is granted by the most powerful form of Lord Shiva, Kaal Bhairav, also fondly referred to as the kotwal or the guardian of Kashi. Legend has it that the aura of Kaal Bhairav is so fierce that even death is afraid of it, and therefore, worshipping Him can wipe out any negativity or unpleasantness from one's life. It is a place where the sun rises, thanks to the magnanimity of Lord Shiva, and sets steeped in the divine mysticism of the holy Ganga aarti—such is the enigma of Varanasi.

Juhi Chawla: When there was nothing, He was omnipresent. When there will be utter emptiness, He will still be there.

For aeons, people have an ingrained belief that there is a mystical power that has tied together so many millions of people. Sometimes with hands raised in faith and sometimes with hands folded in obeisance; sometimes carrying thalis of holy offerings, and at others bearing the holy books in faith—through these, all of us are engaged in a continual search for Him.

I, Juhi Chawla, will take you on such a sojourn, which is a unification of all such feelings, which traverses thousands of miles and draws people to the places where we may find Him. The experience of that faith, this journey, is of the conviction that we will.

The mind is automatically drawn to tranquillity. A pilgrim centre is where God is found.

Devotee 1: I have been to many pilgrim centres, but nowhere has it been like this. The good deeds of many births have accumulated here, how else would it be possible to be born here? If we are coming from the side of Howrah and we catch a glimpse of the semicircular shape of the temple, it feels that now we are safe. This is a feeling that cannot be described.

Devotee 2: I am confident that God exists. I have not seen Him, but I know He is there. If any problem confronts us, we think of the Almighty.

Devotee 3: I can talk to Him and maybe that is why I do not see any problems in life. It seems to me that perhaps my life is the best.

Devotee 4: When I go to Baba, it feels like He absorbs all my problems in Himself; He takes care of everything.

Devotee 5: When confidence and faith in Him grow, He can be seen. There will definitely be results, just try and believe. Close your eyes and meditate. You will definitely see God.

Juhi Chawla: Varanasi, in Uttar Pradesh, is one of the most ancient and revered pilgrim centres in India, which lights up all creation and wraps the heart in its beauty.

Devotee 6: Varanasi is like a lover to me. I love it just as passionately.

Ascetic: Varanasi is in my heart, soul, subconscious and in my thoughts and opinions.

Devotee 7: I was born in Varanasi. I have been in Kashi for fifty-six years. It is very difficult to leave and go anywhere else—because the heart is unwilling to leave this place.

Devotee 8 (elderly man): Kashi is no ordinary place, it is something very special.

Devotee 9: Even the pebbles here remind me of Shankar (Shiva). You will see Shankar in every home.

Devotee 10: Shankar never leaves the place; He is always here.

Juhi Chawla: Varanasi is another name for faith. Here, the morning is Shiva and so is the evening. Those who have wandered in the city's alleys have lost themselves in godliness, piety and history. The turbulent heart merged into the silence of the ascetic.

Devotee 11: There is no desire left in me—my heart is full. I do not get this satisfaction anywhere else.

Devotee 12: When I come here, it feels that everything is bound to be all right. The very fact that I have come here means that it is with the blessings of the Almighty.

Devotee 13: This is an ancient city. There is a meaning to the name 'Kashi', which means light. It glitters.

Devotee 14 (elderly man): Another name for Kashi is Anand Dhawan—there is joy all the time here.

Devotee 15: At the extreme south is the Aasi River and at the extreme north is the Varuna River, and it is from these two that the name Varanasi (Varuna + Aasi) has been derived.

Juhi Chawla: Varanasi, both historically and socially, is regarded as the most ancient city in India. It is believed that Varanasi exists on the prongs of Shiva's trident. After His marriage to Parvati, Shiva had apparently settled down in this city.

Devotee 16: This is the city of Baba Bholenath (Shiva) and this is also regarded as Parvati's in-laws' residence. Shivji Himself resides here. The city is not some man-made construction.

Devotee 17: That is why this is called the Maha Shamshan (The Great Cemetery). Kashi is believed to have the power to confer moksha on anyone.

Devotee 18: The difference between moksha and death is that the latter means just freedom from the body, whereas the former is salvation, freedom from the cycle of rebirth and death. In Varanasi, one can attain moksha. And then there is no rebirth for him or her. Kashi is the only place in the world where even death smiles. In this city, one can actually look forward to death.

Devotee 19: To my mind, this is the only place on earth where death is something joyous. If you tell someone, 'May your death occur in Kashi', the happiness on their face is obvious.

Devotee 20: I remember we used to live here, in Tulsi Ghat. There were a number of dharamshalas (hostel-like accommodation)—eighty-year-old veterans used to come and live here. Their purpose was to welcome death in the city.

Devotee 21: People are dying with the goal of living. I continue to live with the hope of dying. This continuing to live with the hope of dying is the mysticism of Varanasi. Death is the nucleus of the city. The activities of life surround it. Death is the paramour here. That is why when there is a funeral procession, people dance and are joyous.

Juhi Chawla: This pilgrimage is a fusion of life and death. There is such peace and tranquillity in the ambience here that those awake cannot sleep and those suffering attain peace.

Devotee 22: When I am in need, this is where I spend time. Just like one finds solace in a mother's lap, it is the same sense of comfort that I get here. There is a lot of peace here.

Ascetic: When one comes here, one forgets everything—one forgets if the son has got a job, or if the father is suffering from cancer. Ganga Ma takes away your sorrows.

Juhi Chawla: The smooth stony path of the ghat leading to the river has been touched by Shankar's feet. Coming in contact with it, the Ganga seems to have become even holier.

Whenever you take a dip in the holy city, the soul is satiated.

Devotee 23: Whenever faced with any kind of danger, I remember Ganga Ma. Whether anybody has a mother or not, She is the Universal Mother. You can rest assured that She is there. Just go there and imbibe this experience. Your mind will be burden-free and your problems will get resolved.

Devotee 24: Gangaji has come down from the heavens to rescue us. She is chaste. Though we cannot see heaven, we can see Her, and that's enough.

Devotee 25: There is peace while bathing in the Ganga. And only when the heart is at peace can something be done for the Almighty. If you believe, she is Mother Ganga—otherwise she is just flowing water.

Devotee 26: This is Moksha Dham. If you take a dip in the Ganga, you will attain moksha.

Juhi Chawla: Varanasi is not just a pilgrimage centre, but a place to imbibe and understand the twists and turns of life. Devotees come here with a lot of desire and hope—some ask for the boon of life while others come to perform the obsequies of their elders; some look for peace and others come in search of moksha.

Devotee 27: Kashi, Durgaji and Shiva are so integrated that they cannot be separated from one another.

Ascetic: There is a distinct feeling that Shankar Bhagwan is here. He has the trident in His hand, the deer skin on Him, holy ash on His forehead and a serpent around His neck. What a divine picture Shankar paints.

Devotee 28: Nobody can oust Him from my heart. We were in such dire straits, we had nothing at all. But I prayed to Baba Bholenath, meditated and made special offerings to Him, and now with His blessing we have everything.

Devotee 29: If you ask for one, He will give you ten. If you don't ask for anything, He will give you a hundred.

Devotee 30: Benares is about faith and not just belief. If someone says they have heard that one attains moksha in Kashi, that is belief. But if they say, 'In Kashi we attain freedom', that is faith.

Juhi Chawla: It is believed that Shiva in the form of Vishwanath lives in Kashi. But His presence is felt in every corner of the city. A magnetic pull draws millions to this city of Shiva. But the place where this pull is strongest is the Kaal Bhairav Temple, situated 3 km from Kashi.

Devotee 31: This temple is connected to us in such a manner that it seems to be our home.

Devotee 32: The days I am unable to come to this temple, my mind remains disturbed.

Devotee 33: Whenever I come to Baba, it feels as though I have forgotten all my sorrows and problems. It feels that I have left all my tensions behind.

Devotee 34: If there is any inner turbulence or worry, they vanish the moment I see Shiva.

Devotee 35: The feeling is that we can do anything for Him. If someone gives us poison and says that it's Baba's blessed food, we will eat it without any hesitation. It is a manifestation of our faith in Shiva.

Devotee 36: Shiva is so attached to His children that under no circumstances will He leave His children in any kind of pain. If there happens to be any problem, He will take care of it.

Juhi Chawla: The Kaal Bhairav Mandir happens to be one of the oldest in Kashi. This is where one of the most fearsome incarnations of Shiva, the Kaal Bhairav, resides. It was Shiva Himself who was responsible for the advent of Kaal Bhairav. The Lord of time, Kaal Bhairav, was a name given by Shiva Himself.

There's a story associated with this too. Brahma had five disciples and there was a conversation among them about Brahma. One of the disciples spoke in a derogatory manner about Shiva. This greatly angered Shiva and from His third eye Kaal Bhairav was born. The fifth head of Brahma was severed, so he was accused of Brahmahatya, or the killing of Brahma. To atone for this sin Kaal Bhiarav went around the Brahmand, or the universe. Kaal Bhairav then reached Shiva and asked how He would atone for this sin. He was thus sent to Kashi, because that was Shankar Bhagwan's favourite place. On reaching, the head of Brahma, which had had been glued to Him, was dropped into a reservoir and Kaal Bhiarav was seated on a dog and on one finger.

Since then this is where he has been living. That is why He is also known as the kotwal.

Even the wind bows its head in respect before it blows in Kashi. It is mandatory for anyone coming to Kashi to pay their respects to Kaal Bhairav.

Devotee 37: It is clearly stated in the Puranas that whoever comes to Kashi and does not perform the ritualistic worship in His honour does not get salvation or moksha.

Yama, or the God of Death, is not permitted to enter this city. And that is why to punish you for your sins, Kaal Bhairav has been appointed as administrator and protector of this place.

Juhi Chawla: Kaal Bhairav is the representative of death and the creator of time. The name of Bhairav instils fear in Death himself. Anything unholy takes to its heels whenever His name is heard.

Devotee 38: I was very sick and, despite going to many doctors, I wasn't getting well. My children took me to get medicines. I returned home and, while I was sleeping, I felt some water being sprinkled on me. When I awoke, there was no sickness at all. I believe it was Kaal Bhairav Baba who had sprinkled the healing water on me.

Devotee 39: When there is a disaster or chance of an untimely death, it can be averted here.

Devotee 40: If you pray sincerely, all you have asked for will be granted. Childless couples come here to pray and within a year their wish is granted, and they come back to thank the Lord.

Devotee 41: When we stand in front of Baba, it feels as if we are in His house, that we are sitting close to Him and communicating with Him. Baba listens to us and then takes care of our problems.

Devotee 42 (young boy): The emotions one feels when one comes face to face with Baba is indescribable.

Devotee 43: Just one look at Him and all worries vanish. This is the kind of mercy Kaal Bhairav Baba has.

Juhi Chawla: The colour of Kashi is the colour of Shiva. The spirit of sunlight is in the devotional songs. What is submitted to Shiva is Abhang, or incantations in praise of Him.

Devotee 44: This is a strange city—the city of Benares, the soil of Varanasi. Whenever anyone dies, there is a call of 'Har Har Mahadev'. Here in Kashi, we say 'Har Har Mahadev' whenever we are happy—say, during weddings—but we also say 'Har Har Mahadev' when someone dies. This is a strange city of Mahadev.

Devotee 45: Benares is not a city, it is the embodiment of Shiva.

Devotee 46: It is not the fortune of everyone to come to Kashi and neither is it the fortune of everyone to breathe their last here. Those who have been fortunate enough are Shiva themselves.

Devotee 47: I have seen many families who have been coming to Kashi for fifteen–twenty years now. Some have used up all their savings to just come here.

Devotee 48: This is a feeling that cannot really be expressed because it is a connection with the Almighty.

Juhi Chawla: Kashi is Kailash; Shiva is Ganga; Shiva is also Shwaz (breath or life). When the last obsequies are performed, it is Shiva who is the gateway to freedom. Shiva lives in every corner of Kashi. Here, everything—life and death, prayers and incantations, moksha, temples and bathing ghats—are all dedicated to Him. Everything is submitted to the Almighty Shiva.

Benares has an aura of mystery. It is a mystic world. If you are able to understand this mysticism, you will know that coming here is like summiting the Everest—it is the climb itself that is worthwhile.

Juhi Chawla: Ma, please wash me away, make me as transparent and pious as Thee, slipping from Shiva's tresses I will follow You till Kailash. And when You come down to the earth, along with You I too will come to Kashi again.